Have We Possibly Met Before?

And Other Stories

Susanna Piontek

Translated from the German

by Guy Stern

Culicidae
Press, LLC

Ames | Berlin | Gainesville | Rome

Culicidae Press, LLC
918 5th Street
Ames, IA 50010
USA
www.culicidaepress.com

Culicidae
PRESS, LLC
culicidaepress.com

Ames | Berlin | Gainesville | Rome

Some of the stories were previously published in English: "In the
Familiy Way" and "Have We Possibly Met Before?" in *dimension2*,
Volume 9 Number 1/2 (double issue): Voices of Cultural Diversity,
(Contemporary German-English Literature), editor: Ingo Stoehr,
Nacogdoches, Texas, 2007, ISSN 1072-7655. "Ice Cream or
Pudding" in *TRANS-LIT2* Vol. XIII/No.1, Spring 2007 (Journal of
the Society for Contemporary American Literature in German
- SCALG), editors: Irmgard Hunt/Jolyon T. Hughes, 2007, ISSN
1933-5911. "Deceit" in *TRANS-LIT2*, Vol. XIV/Vol.2, Fall 2008
(Journal of the Society for Contemporary American Literature in
German - SCALG), editor: Irmgard Hunt/Jolyon T. Hughes, 2008,
ISSN 1933-5911. "The Woman of His Dreams" in *TRANS-LIT2*,
Vol. XV/1, spring 2009 (Journal of the Society for Contemporary
American Literature in German - SCALG), editor: Irmgard Hunt/
Jolyon T. Hughes, 2009, ISSN 1933-5911.

ISBN: 978-0-578-06595-3

Images © 2005 Anne Karge
Cover image © 2011 Michael Lassel, *Kunstmaler*/painter
Cover design, interior layout, and © 2011 by polytekton.com

Life has no handrails.

Carl Sternheim, *Bürger Schippel*

Table of Contents

Preface

Of Short Stories, the Author, and their Close Partnership

The seventeen short stories presented here in English were first published in Germany. They will, by all indications, arouse the same interest in English-speaking readers as they did for readers familiar with German. In these stories time – our time – appears to be speaking to us. It is, of course, the author who addresses and challenges us and who invites us to join her in her reflections and concerns. Her favorite means of communication is the short story, a late addition to the more traditional prose genres of German literature, such as anecdote, novella and novel. One of the short story's frequently used techniques is the surprise ending. It is also typical for Piontek. It will often take us aback, but we ultimately realize that she has consistently played fair with us. The outcome, in retrospect, appears perfectly logical and the characters' actions consistent.

In making the short story her vehicle, Piontek brings her own individual variations to the genre. In German-speaking countries there was much room for such experimentation, given the Germans' late discovery of the genre. In the wake of the total collapse of the Nazi dictatorship and its aftermath a sobering search began for new, genuine and enduring national values to replace the mendacious ones of the previous twelve years. This general search inspired a parallel quest by German-speaking writers to find a literary form that could come to terms with the trauma of the war and the post-war years. It had to be concise, truthful and capable of closely mirroring reality. It was, in the main, the members of a newly formed writers' association with the name of Group '47 who found the answer to their needs in the short story. Writers such as Heinrich Böll and Günter Grass, both Nobel Prize winners in later years, Günter Kunert, Siegfried Lenz, Wolfdietrich Schnurre and, somewhat later, Gabriele Wohmann embraced the new form and introduced it into all the prevailing media of their time. They often drew upon and developed American and Russian models.

Fixing on the short story was essentially a conscious choice. It suggested itself because it readily accommodated the wrenching memory in fictional form of emotional experiences, especially the suffering and subdued hopes of the immediate past. As Wolfdietrich Schnurre, one of the early adopters of the form, put it: "The reason [for our choice] was the subject matter, the plethora of tormenting experiences dating from the war years. Guilty feelings, accusations of the guilty, despair: they all demanded to be heard. Certainly not in an aesthetically ornate form or by well-defined narrative divisions – they clamored for a form of communication that spilled over breathlessly, concisely, sparsely and warily. So the 'discovery' of the short story came just at the right time." Manfred

Durzak, an early advocate for according the short story its proper recognition as an artistic form, gathered more than twenty such emphatic endorsements by German-speaking writers advocating this new form of prose narrative. Relying both on the theoretical writings of relevant authors and on interviews, Durzak's exemplary research brought forth, in the aggregate, a ringing testimonial to the merits of the recently imported form.

Heinrich Böll, to cite but one example, explained his predilection for the short story quite succinctly: "The short story is my favorite form. I believe it is modern in the basic sense of the word, that is to say it represents our time. It has no tolerance for even the slightest carelessness; it remains my favorite form for yet another reason: it is least amenable to being reduced to a preset mold."

Inevitably those endorsements were accompanied by definitions of the newly discovered form. While they of course vary from author to author in their details, there is surprising agreement on the genre's perceived fundamental characteristics. The short story, these writers conclude, transmits experiences of everyday life in its endless variety. They applauded the fact that it directly addresses the reader because they, too, felt impelled to communicate, so to speak, "face-to-face" with their readership. They felt in tune with the realism of the genre, that it does not shy away from the grayness and dreariness of everyday life, and that it eschews heroic characters and heroic gestures. In a somewhat ironic vein Arno Schmidt added: "A short story should not exceed 50 pages."

Since its emergence the short story has become omnipresent in German-speaking countries. It populates the art sections of newspapers; it shows up in anthologies; it is the focus of literary competitions and authors' readings sponsored by German and Austrian municipalities and literary societies. And it is to be found on reading lists ranging from those of high school classes to graduate programs. Indeed, students of German literature, both in the U.S. and abroad, have made the transition from being critical readers of short stories to creators of new ones, some of them publishable – and eventually published. This happened, in fact, in several of my seminars.

To summarize, the short story has now grown firm roots in German-speaking countries, and it has joined the more traditional prose forms. Susanna Piontek carries on this tradition and expands it.

Following one of her readings she told me that as a child she liked to tell stories to her playmates. Indeed, we sense in her narratives the urge to communicate displayed by her predecessors. Clearly it is not the war that informs her writing, as was the case with the Group '47. She lived during and emerged from a period of time that presented us, in the prescient words of Erich Kästner, with a modicum of freedom, but withheld from us – especially if we look at today's social inequalities – the broader freedom envisioned by so many at the end of World War II.

Thus her protagonists vacillate between anxiety and hope. They are mostly quotidian worries – the very ones you and I encounter every day – that confront her characters. Nothing earthshaking, but an individual catastrophe might occur if the family in the story "Ice Cream or Pudding" continues to travel along its personal highway to obesity. Similarly the hopes and aspirations moving her characters do not upheave the heavens. In the story "Pring's Awakening," her protagonist has all but accepted his steady decline, when a sobering experience shocks him into changing his lifestyle. Piontek nurtures the modest hopes of the average person, about whom her Silesian compatriot, the dramatist Gerhart Hauptmann, remarked: "Every person harbors a longing in his heart." But precisely because her characters do not inhabit the upper regions of their society, either by status or wealth, every reader can immediately identify with them. At times Piontek also evokes more than the world immediately outside our windows. For example, in the story "Children's Destinies" she first unveils the dark side of a child's life within the setting of a German town, but then expands the snapshot into a panorama, a microcosm into a macrocosm. She uses a single hint to expose a similar social wrong in a far-off continent. That widening of her narrative horizon places her, in yet another respect, in the brief tradition of the German short story. Just as the returning war veterans in the stories of Wolfgang Borchert and Heinrich Böll represent alienated veterans everywhere, so Piontek's sorrowful children are legion everywhere.

By her own admission, Piontek has never preoccupied herself with the history or theory of the short story. She consciously ignored those aspects of the genre in order to write spontaneous stories that are more 'felt' than studied. Though Piontek read a wide variety of short stories, both German and foreign, she has modeled herself on no one specifically. Nonetheless, her narratives exemplify the above-cited characteristics. None leave the solid ground of everyday living and of reality except the very last one, which will be discussed later.

Her passion to communicate is everywhere evident in her stories, but you will search in vain for fearless heroes and heroines. A quote from the poet Rainer Maria Rilke readily applies to most of Piontek's characters: "Who speaks of victory? To survive is everything." Admittedly, however, the story "In the Family Way" depicts genuine altruism and self-denial: the heroism, if you will, of people-in-the-average. That story was chosen by readers of the journal *Kurzgeschichten* [Short Stories] as "Story of the Month" in May 2004.

Moreover, the dynamic variability of the short story is constantly in evidence in Piontek's texts. This is also a quality that Böll's above-quoted citation attributes to the genre ("the form… least reducible to a preset mold"). She experiments time and again with the form, testing its elasticity. The protagonist of the story "Have We Possibly Met Before?" is thoroughly dissected, even though Piontek maintains an objective, distant, and uninvolved narrator. Equally revealing is her epistolary story "Deceit," since letter exchanges are or can be the most intimate form of personal communication. Two of the stories in this collection approximate murder mysteries; in both cases the "unfinished past" of the Nazi period drives the action. In the last story, "The Tiny Christmas Bell," Piontek enters an entirely different world. As in a fairy-tale, something enchanting happens. But precisely because of this departure, this leap into the supernatural celebrates the miracle of Christmas.

Her style frequently shifts as well. Piontek takes full advantage of the flexibility of the short story; her variations serve to retard or expedite the unfolding of the plot. Her style also reflects the linguistic vernacular of her characters. For example, she may alternate between highly technical language – note the verbal autopsy in "Pring's Awakening" – and the menacing jargon of a delinquent adolescent in the story "The Evil Child," between the beer-boozy language at a class reunion and the flippant, careless monologue of a repeatedly widowed woman who, despite her calculating wiles, gains our reluctant sympathy. In the story "I Recognized Him Right Away," Piontek moves sure-footedly between three linguistic levels – the fragmentary exchanges typical of a dentist and patient, the pained dialogue between the dentist and her boyfriend, and the silent communication of the troubled woman protagonist, which is somehow made audible by the author.

Piontek's highly individual modes of narration also extend to numerous other aspects of her stories and are equally striking. Her humor accompanies her even when she leads us into a rather gruesome setting or when she describes the demise of one of her characters. A postal clerk takes his leave from this world, marked with a postal stamp indelibly printed on his forehead. Despite her frequent use of sparse, unsentimental language, one intuits subliminally that the fates of her characters profoundly affect her. She is not intent upon imposing lessons on us, yet her feelings of compassion in such stories as "Children's Destinies" are subtly transmitted. Her close involvement with her characters is further borne out by the fact that she is reluctant to simply dismiss her fictional creations into their prior non-existence. Several of them resurface in a subsequent story against a different background that serves to project yet another of their character traits. Respecting her readers as partners, Piontek does not call attention to the fact that a figure has reappeared. She leaves the detecting of these cross connections to each reader's perspicacity. Likewise she relies upon the imagination of her readers when she lets the same motifs serve as the agents of a story's turning point. This happens, for example, when two characters turn up with virtually identical features, leading to a comedy (or tragedy) of errors.

This foreword has been written with the same reticence. Its occasional interpretations are tentative. In the spirit of the short-story genre and of the writer Piontek, who have entered into such a rewarding partnership, each reader is encouraged to find his or her own entrance to these narratives. In short, these short stories tell their own "stories."

Guy Stern   *Wayne State University*

In the Family Way

When Aaron came home that evening, he immediately realized that something was wrong. Everything was quiet. Too quiet. Not the usual yelling of the two girls. Not Hannah's loving but sometimes futile efforts to convince them that it was time to go to bed.

"Hannah?" Aaron asked in the silence. No answer.

Where could they be? He tried to fight down his growing unease. Maybe she and the girls had taken the bus and gone to her parents in Haifa. But at this time of day? As Aaron thought about other possibilities he heard it – the sound of a sob, coming from the bathroom.

"Hannah?" he called again and with a pounding heart he opened the bathroom door. Instantly his glasses steamed up, and he could hardly see anything. His wife was sitting in the bathtub, her dark wet hair plastered to her head, her face red and contorted from crying. Despite the heat, she was shivering.

Aaron took off his glasses and knelt down beside the bathtub. When he put his hand into the water, he let out a startled cry and pulled it out. With tears streaming down her face, Hannah stared into space and said nothing. Again he put his hand into the water slowly, knowing now how hot it was. Even so, it was not easy for him to keep it in the water. He put his hand on her stomach, her swollen hot body, and breathed heavily.

"Hannah, darling, what's the matter with you? Why are you crying? Why is the water so hot? Where are the girls?"

Still she did not look at him. As if she were praying, her body rocked back and forth, back and forth. Aaron could not tell if the pearls that ran down Hannah's cheeks were water, sweat, or tears. They were dripping from her chin and the tip of her nose. Gently he turned her face toward his.

"Please tell me, what's wrong! Please!" A feeling of panic threatened to overwhelm him.

"You must get out of the water. Now. It is much too hot for the baby. Come on!" In order to give his words more weight, he pulled the plug.

The gurgling sound of the water draining away seemed to bring his wife back to reality. In a husky voice she gasped out his name and wildly wrapped her arms around him. Aaron held on to his shivering wife and straightened up, carefully helping her to stand up. Getting out of the bathtub, she leaned heavily on him and finally, panting and still shivering, stood on the blue, cloud-shaped terry carpet.

Strange, Aaron thought, why is the carpet blue and not white like a cloud? At the same time it occurred to him that on children's drawings clouds were often painted blue, while the sky around remained white.

Hannah stood motionless and Aaron started to dry her off, questioning her calmly. He helped her into her bathrobe and put his arm around her shoulders. Gently he helped her to the bedroom. Hannah sat down on the bed and Aaron knelt in front of her, wrapped his arms around her legs and looked at her. Anxiously he asked again:

"Hannah, won't you tell me what's the matter?"

She calmed down little by little but still her body was shivering. Her heavy breasts over the thick abdomen were showing from under the open bathrobe. Hannah's body glowed from the hot water.

Her voice was quiet and rough when she started to speak. The children were at cousin Lea's house some blocks away. In the late afternoon Hannah had come home from work. She had sat down on the couch, drinking a glass of juice. She had just wanted to have a little rest and check the mail before picking up the girls. The envelope had been an innocent white one, and for one moment her heart had stopped beating as she read the name of the sender. She had hardly been able to open the envelope, her hands had been shaking so much. Like a mantra she had repeated the words "Please, no," full of premonition. Three times she had read the letter and still she did not want to believe that it was meant for *her*. Something like that always happens to other people. Not to her. And yet now it was her turn. Her and Aaron's.

Clumsily she had gotten up and phoned her cousin. Withholding the real reason, she had only told Lea that she was not feeling well, and that she would like to be alone to rest for a while. Could the girls stay at Lea's until the evening? Aaron would pick them up then. No, no, she should not worry, everything was okay. The heat and her growing girth had worn her out. She was exhausted, and if she had the chance to have a little rest now, she would probably feel better soon.

Later Hannah and Aaron were surprised at how she had managed to put off her break-down until after the phone call. She asked Aaron to go into the living room to get the letter that she had put back into the envelope. Put back as though she could undo having received it and avert the disaster.

When Aaron had finished reading the letter, he turned pale. The letter dropped to the floor. Again kneeling in front of her, he embraced his wife and pressed his pale face against her thick body. The unborn and much-longed-for son kicked and thrashed in his mother's stomach. What had the hot water done to him?

"I won't let them take him away from me," Hannah whispered. "They can't do that. And if they do, they will not get him alive."

Aaron took her hand and kissed the palm. He heaved a deep sigh as he looked intensely into her eyes.

"You mustn't say this, Hannah. Not even think it. We had a premonition that it would happen like this. Ever since we discovered from the ultrasound that it would be a boy, we've known this was possible. Even if we did not talk about it. We were lucky with the girls. Twice lucky.

But only because they were girls. We're not the only ones who are affected by this."

"But I don't want to give him away!" Almost screaming these words, she laid her hands on her stomach in a protective manner. "I don't want to. I don't want to."

Aaron sat down on the bed beside his wife and took her gently in his arms.

"Please, darling, calm down. It doesn't make any sense. We can't do anything about it. Other people get a letter like this and don't know until the baby is born whether it will be a boy or a girl. We can mentally prepare ourselves. It happened to a colleague of mine and his wife, too. Five years ago."

"And? How did they cope with it?" Hannah whispered.

"Fine," Aaron tried to encourage her. "Much better than they had expected. David has turned out really well. Recently I talked to Eliezer about it. Believe me, after a while you don't think of it any more. Again and again people tell him how much David looks like him. Hardly any one knows that he is one of these exchange children.

Hannah, please remember how we ourselves saw the whole thing a few years ago. This law was passed by majority decision. Do you remember how people shouted with joy when the Palestinians gave their consent? And you have to admit that it works. This, and the retreat from the occupied areas, finally brought us peace. Now we've been picked to make the sacrifice. Hannah, we will have a son; we will raise and love him the same way we love our daughters. And in the same way a Palestinian family will love our son. Believe me. The living conditions over there have improved so much in recent years. It is our contribution to peace. Try to see it that way. In the meantime thousands of boys have been exchanged after birth. They are all doves of peace. See it that way, Hannah. There are no assassinations any more. The hatred has subsided. We are all too afraid that we may kill our own sons. On both sides."

Tired, Hannah had put her head on Aaron's shoulder. The baby did not thrash around so much anymore; she felt a calmness coming over her.

Great Assumptions

"And then he proposed to me." Mrs. Caspari let this sentence melt upon her tongue. Her light gray eyes were fixed on Lotte, expectantly. That was the way it always went. Mrs. Caspari inserted a pause for dramatic effect, waited until Lotte had commented or asked a question, and then continued to talk for a few minutes, until the next pause.

"What year was that again?" Lotte asked politely. "1962, the third of June. It was on a Monday, and Pope John the XXIII died that day, of stomach cancer, the poor man. Of course, as a good Catholic woman you can't forget a day like that."

Mrs. Caspari had reached the third marriage in her narrative. In about ten minutes she would start on the death of her only child. Then another demonstration of attentiveness would be appropriate. Meanwhile, Lotte allowed her thoughts to roam. She was good at this: to look focused and yet be somewhere else entirely in her thoughts. Word fragments cut through to her ears as if she wore cotton earplugs, and she made an effort to smile.

Good God, how often she had heard these stories by now! How often had she been at Mrs. Caspari's anyway?

At some point Lotte had stopped counting. Mrs. Caspari was a particularly hard nut to crack, and Lotte asked herself how long she was supposed to go on like this. With all the others it had worked better; with them she had been more successful, but how aptly it is said: haste makes waste. Besides, in this case, it would really pay off.

Mrs. Caspari had managed the feat of marrying profitably four times, and of surviving all her husbands. Lotte would have loved to do likewise, but for that she was too ungainly. Only a few men had taken an interest in her when she was younger, but Lotte didn't think any of them were good enough for her. The first one was too short, the second one a vegetarian, and the third one was attached to his mother's apron strings. But above all they had one thing in common: all of them were as poor as church mice; in short, for Lotte they were ciphers. You only lived once and you should shape your life as comfortably and pleasantly as possible. Mrs. Caspari groped for a small white-lace handkerchief and dabbed tears from her cheeks. Lotte prepared herself for her re-entry into the conversation.

"Michael was such a good boy. His professors were so pleased with him. No doubt he would have become a wonderful physician, just like his father."

Lotte nodded sorrowfully and softly felt for Mrs. Caspari's hand. Lovingly she stroked the large aquamarine in its flashy gold setting and pondered how the ring would look on her own hand.

"How long had your son been at the university when he had that car accident?"

Once more Lotte pressed her hand in sympathy. From now on it would take about a quarter of an hour until Mrs. Caspari would start talking about the death of her third husband. Lotte suppressed a yawn and mulled over what kind of canned soup to buy on her way home. Pea soup, or maybe bean soup. She also needed potato chips, candy, and soda for her lonely evenings at home. Her TV set had finally given up the ghost for good over the weekend. She would have to go to the welfare office this week in order to apply for money for a new one.

Lotte once again felt a surge of impatience and forced herself to stay calm. In the case of Mrs. Kampmann in the St. Ann Old Age Home it had taken almost a year until she had given Lotte the pearl necklace. The jeweler had given her 300 Euros for it, and she was able to live in the lap of luxury for a few days. She bought herself champagne and expensive perfume, a black skirt and a sky-blue silk blouse, and, in a department store, a cheap pearl necklace which, at first glance, looked like Mrs. Kampmann's. She had eaten at good restaurants; they had served portions far too small on plates much too large, and Lotte had tried to appear as though she were used to dining so exquisitely every evening. On these occasions she would look fur-tively around and, out of the corner of her eye, size up the other guests in the restaurant.

At the conclusion of her few visits to the restaurant, Lotte would dig for the wallet in her threadbare imitation leather handbag and pay her bill without ever leaving a tip. That would come later, when she had more money.

Beneath the waiter's contemptuous looks and with sweaty spots under her armpits, she would leave the restaurant with the grandest dignity her body weight would permit, and start on her way home on tired, heavy legs.

The small apartment under the roof was unbearably hot during the summer months, and Lotte tried to spend most of the daytime in two air-conditioned assisted-living homes and in the shady park. She returned home only in the evening hours; the sticky heat took her breath away and she let herself fall on the couch where she remained lying like a beached walrus. Gasping and fanning herself with advertising brochures she awaited the cool of the night. But the most suspenseful movie, the coolest soda, and the sweetest candy could only distract her momentarily from her discontent. Why did life have to be so unfair?

"Just imagine, dear Lotte, I met Otto, of all places, at Alfred's grave. He was kind enough to drive Alfred's cousin to the cemetery when her car wouldn't start." Mrs. Caspari's bluish tinted curls trembled softly.

"Yes, Mrs. Caspari, fate often works in curious ways." Lotte's glance strayed to the massive gold chain that scarcely showed itself to best advantage on the wrinkled neck of the old woman. The chain must have cost a fortune! Again, interminable minutes were devoted to husband number four who had worshiped and spoiled her in every way imaginable.

Lotte felt uncomfortable, not only because of Mrs. Caspari's boring stories that she, by now, knew almost by heart. The atmosphere in the small room at the end of the hallway depressed her. Heavy oak furniture, a dark carpet of undefinable color, several family photos on faded wallpaper, a horrible etching showing a boat onshore in front of a clouded sky, two Hummel figurines, a yellow plastic rose in a narrow crystal vase, and above it all the smell of an old parchment-colored woman who was no longer particularly concerned with cleanliness. The smell mingled with Lotte's own perspiration and made breathing difficult.

With an unsteady hand Mrs. Caspari reached out for the bottle of mineral water on the small table. Carefully Lotte took the bottle from her hand, removed the cap, and poured the already stale water into a glass. Mrs. Caspari blinked at her gratefully. Lotte clumsily lifted herself from the armchair, pushed her hands into the small of her back and turned her body, with its lack of a waistline, slowly from one side to the other.

"That's a beautiful picture you have there, Mrs. Caspari."

"Oh, I'm glad you like it, Lotte dear. My second husband, Michael's father, gave it to me as a gift. We used to drive to Cuxhaven for a few days every year. It was so beautiful, taking a walk along the coast. One day I discovered this etching in a small store. And because I liked it so much, my husband absolutely had to buy it for me, even though it was anything but inexpensive. But Oskar, you see, couldn't deny me anything. I only had to say that I liked something, and immediately he bought it for me. Have you ever been to Cuxhaven, my dear child?"

"No, but if it's so beautiful, I will definitely go there someday." Lotte looked at her wristwatch.

"You must do that by all means, my dear. You know, you can't imagine what immense pleasure your visits give me. If one is my age and has nobody anymore in this whole wide world, one is really badly off. And for that reason I always so look forward to Tuesday, when I know that you are coming to visit." Mrs. Caspari paused for effect and smiled meaningfully. "Really, my dear, it won't be to your disadvantage that you devote so much of your precious time to me."

A shock of pure joy flashed through Lotte. Mrs. Caspari, too, had painfully raised herself from her armchair. With her left hand she leaned on her cane. The right hand she extended to Lotte.

"I'll walk you to the door. You'll come again next Tuesday, won't you?" She had slipped her arm through Lotte's and was taking small unsteady steps.

"Of course, Mrs. Caspari. I'm truly sorry that I don't have more time. You always tell such interesting stories and I could listen to you for hours. So, let me wish you the best for the coming week. I'll see you again next Tuesday at three."

Lotte threw Mrs. Caspari a final long, loving smile before she closed the door behind her. In the corridor she leaned with her back against the wall for a few moments, closed her eyes, and breathed deeply.

"Good evening. Does the heat bother you so much, too?" Lotte gave a start. She looked into the friendly face of nurse Laura who, with her freshly starched smock, appeared to spread a breath of cool air. Laura was on the way to Mrs. Caspari. Lotte smiled at her and murmured a reply.

On the first floor, near the exit, a woman she had seen several times before walking busily along the corridor, caught her attention. Actually, it wasn't really a woman, but rather a lady. She was tall, had short blond hair, a good figure, and always wore an elegant dress or suit. She was roughly Lotte's age.

Once she had reached the street, Lotte looked up once more to the third floor, but today old Mrs. Caspari was not standing at the window, waving. She was probably being cared for by the nurse.

At home Lotte made herself comfortable. She undressed, washed herself, and then slipped into the lilac-colored bathrobe Mrs. Gerhardt had given her. She lived in the same assisted-living home from which Lotte had just returned, but in another wing. Thursday afternoons were devoted to her. Mrs. Gerhardt was not quite as old as Mrs. Caspari. Besides, she had far less money than the four-time widow, but had so far been much more gener-ous. On Lotte's birthday and at Christmas Mrs. Gerhardt had slipped her a one-hundred Euro bill, and occasionally she gave Lotte some old clothing or a box of chocolates.

In her thoughts Lotte relived the afternoon once more. What was it that Mrs. Caspari had said shortly before Lotte had left? "It won't be to your disadvantage that you are giving me your precious time." And how she had smiled saying that!

Lotte sighed and shoved two chocolates into her mouth at the same time. Mrs. Caspari was already in her mid-eighties and in precarious health. A few weeks ago she had told Lotte that she owned a house, which she had rented out, at the edge of the city. And since that moment Lotte could think of nothing else. Should she perhaps visit Mrs. Caspari on Sundays as well? It wouldn't last long anyway, and Lotte didn't want to have to reproach herself later on.

The next Sunday Lotte stood once again in front of Mrs. Caspari's door, holding some hand-picked wild flowers. No response when she knocked. Slowly she pushed down the door handle. The door was locked. In the nurse's wardroom Laura stood leaning against the kitchen cupboard and was leafing through a magazine. When Lotte entered, she looked up. "You surely wanted to visit Mrs. Caspari, right?"

"Yes, but the door ..." Lotte stammered and pressed the flowers against her enormous chest. Nurse Laura put the magazine aside, went up to Lotte and put a hand on her arm. "Mrs. Caspari died Friday night," she said compassionately. "Please go down to see our director, Mrs. Pauli, on the first floor, room 8. She told me to send you to her when I saw you."

As if in a trance, Lotte moved toward the elevator. She had been waiting for this moment – but she had not counted on its coming so soon. The closer she came to the door of the director's office, the faster her heart pounded. She nervously ran her fingers through her hair and breathed in deeply before knocking. Instead of the expected "come in," the door was briskly opened and Mrs. Pauli looked first at Lotte and then at the flowers before she made an inviting gesture. "Please, do come in." Today the director was wearing a lime green suit and her lips shimmered in a pale pink. Lotte still held the flowers pressed to her chest as she sat down on the light-colored wicker chair.

"My name is Kessler, Lotte Kessler. I wanted to visit Mrs. Caspari and nurse Laura told me that ..." Lotte faltered and Ms. Pauli took up the conversation.

"I've asked you to see me in order to carry out a wish of Mrs. Caspari's. When nurse Laura went to help her get up yesterday morning, Mrs. Caspari was dead already. She had died in her sleep. In her night table drawer we found a letter, simply addressed to 'Lotte'. Since we didn't know your last name, we unfortunately could not phone you."

"That would not have been possible anyway because I don't have a telephone," Lotte replied in a flat voice.

"Oh, I see. Well, at any rate, here is the letter for you. Do you want to read it right away?"

Mrs. Pauli held the letter out to Lotte, who placed the flowers on Mrs. Pauli's desk and tore open the envelope.

Meanwhile the director of the assisted-living home tactfully bent over some documents.

The handwriting was scrawled and as tiny as Mrs. Caspari herself had been. The letter had been written on Thursday. Now everything would be decided. For one brief moment Lotte saw herself furnishing a house, herself decked out with precious jewelry, in a lime green suit and lighter by at least 80 pounds.

Dear Lotte,

No one knows when one's last hour will strike, but at my age you have to reckon with it every day because you're standing closer to your Lord than you would like. I want to thank you, my dear, for spending so much time with me. You can't imagine how much pleasure it gave me to chat with you. Do you still remember how you started talking to me in the park a year ago? I could scarcely believe my good fortune when you asked me whether you could visit me sometimes. A person who pays attention to the prattle of an old bag! What a gift! The good Lord will repay you, Lotte dear. Unfortunately, I can't show my appreciation as I would like to. I am only a poor old woman. I had the impression that you really liked the etching. Be so kind, Lotte, and take it as a gift and in memory of a lonely person into whose last months of life you brought so much light. I don't have much strength left, but I hope that a few lovely Tuesday afternoons will be granted to us.

In friendship and with gratitude, your Rosalyn Caspari.

The letter dropped into Lotte's lap; all color had drained from her face. *Nothing! All in vain!*

Only a damned etching, which was so ugly that even as a gift Lotte wouldn't have wanted it. Mrs. Pauli's voice tore Lotte out of her state of shock. "Don't you feel well, Mrs. Kessler? May I offer you a glass of water? I am so sorry."

With wet eyes Lotte looked at the director. Tears of disappointment ran down her round cheeks.

"What will become …" Lotte cleared her throat and looked for a handkerchief inside her worn-smooth handbag. "What will become of Mrs. Caspari's property now?" she finally asked bravely.

Mrs. Pauli looked up, astonished.

"Property? Mrs. Caspari was not well off. She had only a small pension. The state covered the room rent in this home."

"But the house she was talking about and the jewelry! I myself saw the gold chain and the ring with a light blue stone." Lotte sobbed, beginning to approach hysteria.

"I am sorry, Mrs. Kessler, but Mrs. Caspari did not own a house."

Mrs. Pauli brought her fingertips together and searched for the right words. "To be sure, I wouldn't be surprised if Mrs. Caspari told you things like that," she added cautiously. "You see, Mrs. Caspari – how shall I put it – was a bit odd. You had to take what she said with a grain of salt. In the beginning when she came to us, she talked of her various marriages and her son; but the fact is she was never married and also had no children. Perhaps she wanted to appear interesting to you to make sure that you would come back. And as far as the jewelry that you mentioned is concerned: for several years she has been living next door with Mrs. Hartung, a rather well-to-do old lady. The two seemed to like each other quite a bit. At any rate, Mrs. Hartung is very distressed about the death of her neighbor. She asked me to return to her the ring and the chain which she had lent to Mrs. Caspari about a year ago for an indefinite period. Mrs. Caspari had begged her for that so fervently that she couldn't turn her down. Yesterday evening I returned the jewelry to her. Mrs. Hartung's initials are on both pieces. Everything is in order."

Compassionately Mrs. Pauli kept quiet. Lotte noisily blew her nose once more, then got up with some effort. Silently she extended her hand to Mrs. Pauli, grasped for the flowers on the desk, and slowly left the room.

In the hallway she breathed deeply, stroked her hair with a tidying gesture, and awkwardly tried to arrange the half-wilted bouquet in a way that would make it look still presentable.

With an immense effort she lifted her spirits, and moved toward the elevator, a determined smile playing on her lips. Mrs. Hartung would surely be happy about her condolence visit.

Pring's Awakening

You don't need to own a pet in order to have a tomcat.*

One can avoid a hangover in various ways: one of them is total abstinence. Another is to be a moderate drinker. That means stopping in time, so that a hangover never occurs. But finally you can keep your intake of alcohol at such a level that you don't give a hangover even a chance, simply because sobriety never sets in.

For the past four years Dr. Herbert Pring belonged to the group of people in the last category. In the army he had learned to drink and other things which, in popular opinion, make a real man out of you. After his time in the service he had studied medicine at Homburg University.

Most medical students are happy when their courses in pathology and forensic medicine are behind them, and prefer devoting themselves to those subjects which deal with curing sick people. But during his studies Pring had discovered that working with dead bodies satisfied him more than with living ones. A dead body can't deceive a

---

Translator's note: The German word for 'tomcat' (*Kater*) also means, colloquially, 'hangover.'

doctor. It speaks for itself. Pring also found it reassuring that no patient could come to harm through his medical handiwork.

When he decided to become a forensic doctor, he had to overcome two obstacles. In both cases alcohol helped him. The first one was the battle against the stench, yes stench, for smell is a word too refined for the rhinal tortures occasioned by inhaling formaldehyde and the reek that rose up from the dead bodies after he had cut them open from throat to pubic bone. The intensity of the stench depends on the degree of putrefaction, but also on profane matters such as the food which the person had ingested shortly before death. Of course, the manner of death also plays a role. For example a drowned corpse with pea soup in its intestines can be more easily endured with a higher level of alcohol.

As to the second obstacle, Pring had not been able to overcome it in more than twenty years, and he knew it was the same with his colleagues. When autopsying children, especially babies, his usual routine abandoned him and each incision into the small cold bodies caused him pain and nausea.

Pring's only child had died of bone cancer four years ago. After that he had become an occasional drinker. He didn't skip a single occasion to hit the bottle, as though his life depended on it. Somehow he managed to continue performing his work so that it could still be considered conscientious. The omnipresent formaldehyde mixed with the emanations from his alcohol-dependent body.

The stinking protective film began to evaporate to some extent only during vacations.

After the death of his child his marriage had gone downhill. He boozed and she mourned, intermittently reproached him, and threatened to leave him. Six months ago she had moved out and filed for divorce.

At this point the thought of putting an end to his life had occurred to Pring for the first time. He drifted, pondered occasionally about the safest way, and waited for the right moment. That would come when his disgust with himself had escalated even more. After his wife had left him, his thoughts acquired more concrete forms. His work worsened. More and more often the small oscillating saw or the scalpel trembled in his hand. Occasionally he was no longer able to go to work. The time was approaching to carry out his intentions.

One afternoon Pring was standing at the dissecting table preparing an autopsy on the last corpse for that day. As always in cases where the cause of death was unknown, the district attorney was present. Pring forced a laugh at the trite little jokes of the jurist, a hardboiled, obese chain smoker, whose secretary was sitting at a small table, ready to feed into a laptop whatever Pring dictated during the post mortem.

The unidentified corpse was wheeled in. A man, 6'-1", 150 pounds, about 50 years of age, Caucasian, found in a forest by a mushroom hunter.

While Pring was still looking at the index card with its cryptic entries, he noticed how the district attorney fell

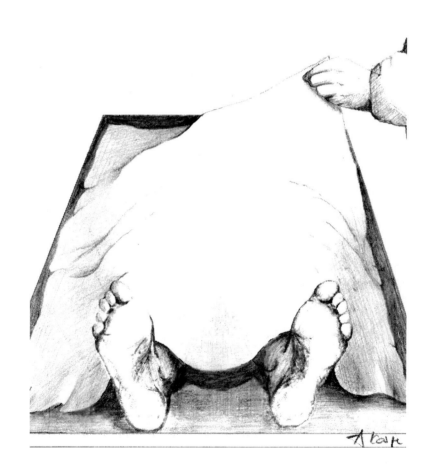

silent in the middle of a sentence. Annoyed, he glanced at the corpulent jurist who, astonished and startled, stared first at Pring and then at the corpse. Now Pring also peered at the dead body and froze.

"My God, what a resemblance," the attorney gasped hoarsely. "One would think it was you lying on that table, or …" he added, "your twin, if you have one."

Pring gulped. He was seeing how he would look if he were to commit suicide. This unknown man was his spitting image. Driven by a sudden impulse he turned up the right arm of the dead man and glanced at the inside of the upper arm, about four inches above the elbow. With a soft cry he let go and staggered. On that spot was a large birthmark in the form of a butterfly.

Exactly like his.

On that very same evening Pring sat, for the first time, in the circle of Alcoholics Anonymous.

Certainty

She is tired. Very tired. She sits in her small kitchen at the white-varnished wooden table, and waits. So tired that she has indeed forgotten that she is waiting.

Her feet are cold, as always. She has nestled her heavy head between both her hands, her thumbs sticking out into the air like two miniature antennas. The skin on her elbows is red and raw – that's good because it keeps them from sliding apart. She wants to keep her eyes open, but can manage that for only a few seconds. Then behind closed lids her eyes rotate inward and she can see inside herself.

She's been waiting for him for an hour. The small kitchen smells of the food she has cooked for him. Indian chicken curry. He really enjoys that. She cut the recipe out of a magazine but has altered it to suit herself. The cinnamon in her kitchen does not come out of a shaker – she uses whole sticks of cinnamon. She also adds cardamom, pressing open a seed capsule and liberating the small pieces, which cling closely together as though they were afraid to be separated.

Sometimes she chews on a piece of cardamom. The taste calms her down, and her breath smells better than if she had used the best toothpaste.

She hates to cook, but he does not know that. When he comes to her, he sits down at the varnished wooden table and eats what she has prepared for him.

The chicken curry has turned cold. A skin like that on hot milk has formed on top of the yellow sauce. A cinnamon stick pokes up like a dead tree trunk out of a swamp.

The crowning touch of a good chicken curry, indeed for any meal she cooks for him, is her secret. Invisible, odorless, tasteless, yet present nonetheless.

Good he doesn't know that she spits once into every meal she prepares for him.

She does so with reverence, a spoon in one hand, while holding onto her hair with the other, so that not a single strand falls into the food when she bends over pot or pan. As an added ingredient a small amount suffices, a thread from her lips to the food, streaked with transparent little bubbles. And even if it is only a droplet: with it she surrenders herself.

When he eats, he also ingests something of her, he also has her in his mouth, his gullet, his stomach.

She likes that thought. She wants to be part of him and this way it's so simple.

She hates to cook, but what is far worse is to watch him eat – or, rather, to have to listen to him eating. She doesn't mind how he mingles his words with the food, words which then leave his mouth imbued with a certain smell.

No, it's the noises emanating from his eating that make her nervous. The grinding of his jaws. The tongue-propelled shuffling of the food from one side to the other, then the swallowing. The swallowing is the worst of it, even though it looks good when his Adam's apple bounces up and down.

He has been coming for years now. When he arrives they sit opposite each other in the small kitchen. Neither one speaks. She sits there and watches him while he eats. She never eats with him. She only eats when she is alone. No one has ever seen her eating, only drinking.

Her second secret is the balls of wax she places in her ears whenever he eats. She likes to watch him eat; she only dislikes hearing him. She's fascinated by the appearance of an opening fold in his face and how the food, lying before him on a plate, disappears into his head.

In the early days he would speak while eating, insecure and embarrassed, because he had to eat by himself. Confused, because she never said anything. In the end he kept silent and simply ate. She liked that best of all. One can still talk after eating. Then she can hear again too, because she has inconspicuously removed the balls of wax from her ears.

When she has cleared the table, she is ready to listen. About stress with his boss, arguments with his wife, aches and pains since his operation, trouble with the tax office.

From time to time she says something, and what she says is not important. It isn't that it is stupid or inappropriate, but it doesn't matter greatly. She listens and that is important. She has attained mastery in that.

Unnoticed by him she imitates his bearing. If he reaches for his glass she does likewise. They light their cigarettes almost simultaneously or cross their legs. In her case it takes a little longer, until she has placed her one stiff leg across the other. With both hands. The simultaneous actions arouse in him a feeling of closeness and solidarity. Aside from the spittle, but that he doesn't know about, of course.

It's late. He won't come today, even though he had promised. She overcomes her tiredness, gets up with a sigh and turns on the kitchen stove. Taking up a fork she removes the yellow skin and the cinnamon tree trunk.

Before starting to eat she takes the calendar down from the wall. It comes from a pharmacy with a primitive painting. It hangs on the wall, level with his head. When he sits opposite her, she can't see the calendar.

From the adjoining room she fetches the round mirror with the black-painted wooden frame. On its back is a small hole for a nail. She hangs up the mirror on the spot where the calendar is usually placed.

Then she resumes her place and looks earnestly and attentively into her own eyes. Her meal, steaming, is standing in front of her. Before she takes the first forkful to her mouth, she stuffs up her ears with the balls of wax.

He'll be back again tomorrow. That she knows for sure.

Have We Possibly Met Before?

It was a bright and sunny May day in 1980.

Albert Faber, his back to the wall, was sitting in a corner of the coffeehouse. On the table in front of him were a vase holding a genuine rose, a cup of Irish coffee, a glass of mineral water, a case for his glasses, and an ashtray filled with cigarette butts. He appeared to be reading a business newspaper.

His suit was of good quality, his shirt and shoes no less. A conservatively patterned silk tie harmonized to a tee with the color scheme of his suit. Despite his advanced age, Faber sat upright in his chair. White hair framed a well-formed head. His eyes, like those of many older people, displayed no distinct color; they gleamed moistly out of their deep sockets. Above thin lips sprouted the mere hint of a whitish mustache. His sunburned pate was dotted with age spots, as were his powerful hands, which drew the newspaper close to his face. From the little finger of his left hand a signet ring sparkled brightly.

Faber seemed to be restless. Time and again he surreptitiously glanced over the rims of his glasses and above

the newspaper into the spacious room and let his gaze wander over the other guests.

The coffeehouse was stylishly furnished. Its atmosphere wavered between jejune and discriminating in taste; as a result, the room reflected both. Its ambiance of sophistication was topped off by subdued teahouse music, precious china, and the staff's discreet and polite service.

Faber looked up when he heard the melodious laughter of a woman being helped out of her coat by a waiter. After a short exchange between the two, the woman headed for a small table in Faber's vicinity. Her dark hair spread in elegant waves over the collar of her suit. A hint of expensive perfume filled his nostrils. He refolded his newspaper.

She sat in such a way that he could observe her out of the corner of his eye without drawing attention to himself. He liked what he saw. Faber took a sip from his cup and lit a cigarette. The woman glanced briefly in his direction before becoming absorbed in the menu. After finishing his cigarette, Faber stubbed it out energetically in the ashtray and got up. Not taking his eyes off the woman for a moment he made a direct line to her table. He clicked his heels almost inaudibly, like an old Prussian officer, and bowed slightly. She looked up at him, visibly surprised.

"Please excuse me, madam, if I take the liberty of addressing you." He let a moment elapse and then looked at her, his face earnest. "You look very familiar to me. Have we possibly met before?"

Smiling in a friendly manner, she looked at him closely.

"I don't think so. Where could we have met?" Faber took a deep breath.

"Well, I can't say either, but somehow you look remarkably familiar to me. Did you ever live in Berlin?"

Even before she could answer, Faber politely asked whether he might join her.

"No," she answered. Her smile had disappeared. "I never lived in Berlin and, no, you decidedly may not join me. Please excuse me now, I am expecting someone."

She had scarcely finished her last sentence when a young woman approached the table, bags from a boutique shop rustling in her hand. While still a few tables away, she greeted the seated woman with an affectionate "Hello, Mom."

Faber ventured another bow, mumbled an apology, and without delay returned to his table. As he was paying for his drinks, he noticed that the young woman turned around to look curiously at him and, giggling, said something to her mother. Ramrod-stiff and slightly offended, he left the coffeehouse, not neglecting to extend another polite nod in their direction.

Of course he did not know the woman, but occasionally the little trick worked. Now and again he had succeeded in striking up a closer acquaintance in this manner.

One week later Faber was occupying a table in another elegant coffeehouse while covertly observing the guests. He was quite repelled by the realization that he was the object of inviting glances from an older woman whose hefty breasts could scarcely be restrained by the buttons of her sky-blue blouse. Faber was just mulling over what a person of that type was doing in a sophisticated place like this when a woman in a hat caught his attention.

Some years younger than he and exceedingly well-groomed, she had an intelligent-looking, beautiful face, which was dominated by large, almost black eyes.

Faber sprang to his feet, straightened his back and approached the table occupied by the woman. This time he would vary his approach.

"May I sit down at your table for a moment?"

The woman stared at him. Faber interpreted her silence as a form of consent and sat down opposite her.

"Please tell me, madam, have we possibly met before?" He threw her an ingratiating smile.

It annoyed him that she still said nothing and continued to stare at him with wide open eyes. He had just decided on his next question, when it suddenly flashed through his mind that he had indeed seen this face before. Despite the fact that she was a stranger, she seemed nevertheless somehow familiar.

"I have the feeling that we may have known each other before. Have you ever lived in Berlin?"

She swallowed, clearing her throat while fighting for an answer.

"Yes, at an earlier time I used to live in Berlin."

Her answer came so softly that Faber had trouble understanding her. A broad, jovial smile spread across his wrinkled face.

"Well, don't you see, it immediately crossed my mind, you have seen that beautiful woman somewhere before. If I only knew ..."

He forced his face into a pensive expression and tried to remember. Was it possible that he really did know her? But if so, from where?

"I do think we know each other!" She intended her voice to be firm, but did not succeed. "However, we didn't know each other in Berlin."

By now, the horrified expression in the woman's eyes was underscored as her face turned pale. Faber swallowed a few times, suddenly feeling unsettled. His hands were moist, and he furtively wiped them on his trousers.

"Don't you think it is quite hot in here?" the woman asked in a brittle voice as she began with trembling hands to roll up the sleeves of her blouse.

"Not really ..." Faber answered, confused and hesitating. He felt his heart beating loudly, the blood resounding in his ears, as his anxiety rose.

He stared at her, and, with a mixture of consternation and fascination, thought he detected hatred in her eyes. There was something amiss with her. Something at odds with her entire appearance. Then as if struck by lightning, it became clear to him from where he knew her. The numbers told the story. The faded numbers, tatooed on her lower arm.

Children's Destinies

After buying a bus ticket, I looked around for a seat. Many of them were already taken, but I spotted two adjoining seats in the back of the bus. They were located directly behind the two seats abutting the open space. In every public bus there is one open space opposite the rear door, where one can place bicycles, for example. The twin seats directly next to it are ideally suited for someone who wants to keep an eye on, say, a baby carriage because he or she can even hold on to it by the handle.

In fact, in that space, a pram or rather a buggy was standing, in which a little girl was seated. Apparently the two adults sitting in front of me were the parents. The woman was probably in her late twenties; the man some years younger. She was tall and considerably overweight. Medium-brown greasy hair clung to her head. She had squeezed herself into light-grey leggings and a sleeveless red t-shirt. The man was slender, wore jeans and a t-shirt with an advertising slogan. His head was shaved bald, and his eyebrows pierced by several metal rings. One could

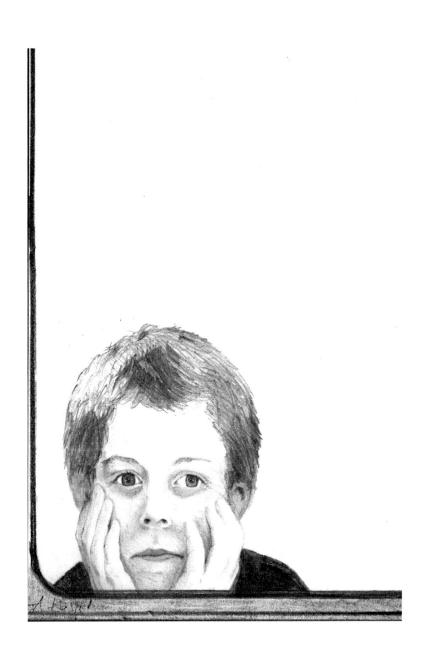

spot a variety of tattoos on his lower arms. A strong smell of cigarettes, alcohol, and sweat assaulted my nose.

I was just thinking about changing my seat when a boy from the rear section of the bus passed me and sat down on an auxiliary seat at the other end of the open space. Why on earth wasn't he in school? When I saw his face, I was profoundly startled. He couldn't have been more than eight or nine years of age, but he had an old, tortured face. Beneath his eyes were deep, dark rings, which emphasized even more the pronounced pallor of his skin. His facial expression evinced great worry, if not desperation. His forehead was lined with deep furrows of sorrow, and these furrows did not disappear even when he looked out of the bus window, supporting his chiseled chin with his hand. Like a prisoner who is aware of the hopelessness of his situation, his glance traveled back and forth between the two adults. They paid no attention to him at all, and I was not sure whether they and the boy belonged to one another. Besides, the man appeared too young to me to be the biological father of the boy. Only when the boy briefly stroked the girl's hair from behind did I know that he was part of the family. This tender gesture, which probably had not lasted more than two seconds, was upsetting to me, and I was imagining how much his subconscious was crying out for a caring and loving gesture like that himself. Even at that moment his forehead scarcely relaxed.

The little sister did not react to the fleeting caress. Moreover, the adults had no glance to spare for that child either, a transparent, pale girl of about twenty months. The little one sat motionless in her buggy and sucked heavily on a pacifier. She kept perfectly quiet and with a serious mien gazed at the man and the woman.

Other children her age move in lively fashion, smile at their parents and wait for a loving glance while they curiously explore their surroundings. Or they whine or cry, desiring the undivided attention of those who are responsible for them.

This girl was different. It appeared as if some inner wisdom prompted her to keep absolutely still. Yet perhaps it was not an inner wisdom but horrible experiences that had caused this tiny human being, just like her older brother, to fall silent at an early age. There are times when one can survive only if one knows how to make oneself nearly invisible. Some children have to learn that when they are still in the womb of their mothers.

I remembered having read, many years ago, a report about child labor in Colombia. Even the smallest child had to work in mines and quarries. I shall never forget the deeply furrowed hand of a five-year old who had been photographed close-up. Every day he had to perform heavy manual labor for about twelve hours in order to support his family. His life expectancy was less than thirty years. The dirty hand was thick-skinned and rough; a thick callus was clearly visible. And yet this hand belonged to a small child, to a boy who would never have the chance for a different existence. Pity and rage had caused me to cry.

And now I felt similarly, as I was watching the boy on the bus. Such sadness suffused his face that it constricted my heart. Anxiously I sought an opportunity to speak at least briefly to this child. There was none.

After a few more stops the family finally got off the bus. With great effort the woman heaved her more than three hundred pounds out of the bus and then helped the man to lift the buggy with its stern content onto the street. I tried to intercept the boy's glance, I wanted at least to smile at him. But during the entire journey he had not even looked at me.

I Recognized Him Right Away

Miriam yanked the door to the second treatment room. Just one more patient and she could look forward to a well-deserved weekend with Robert. The gaunt elderly man in the dentist's chair was staring at her out of his dark eyes, faintly smiling.

"Good afternoon," Miriam greeted the new patient. A bony hand took a hold of hers. "Good afternoon. My name is Winterstein."

Every bit of color vanished from Miriam's face. She looked away from him and turned to his medical record, which her assistant Irene had placed on top of the filing cabinet. The record listed him as Albert Winterstein, together with his date of birth and his address.

Miriam felt nausea welling up inside her. Still looking at his record and avoiding his glance, she tried to make her voice sound normal.

"What can I do for you, Mr. Winterstein?"

"When I was eating yesterday, a piece of a filling broke off. It left quite a gap. Just so you know I haven't visited a dentist for several years."

Miriam took a deep breath. Her heart was beating hard and fast. Slowly she sat down on the revolving chair and reluctantly bent over Winterstein who had already opened his mouth wide. With a routine glance she inspected his teeth before asking him whether he wanted an injection. He declined, and she began her work with her customary care. She made sure that her hand motions were completely steady, being anxiously mindful that neither Winterstein nor Irene should detect her inner turmoil.

As she finished the treatment, her glance passed over his almost grey, wavy hair and his dark eyes. "You need an additional filling. The last molar on the upper right side doesn't look good at all. Please make an appointment for a time near the end of the month."

"I'll be gone by then. Very soon I'll be off to America for an extended period. Could I perhaps get an appointment for next week?"

Miriam had already straightened up. "Yes, but in that case you will have to plan on waiting for some time."

"All right. And goodbye, Doctor."

Once more she felt her hand enclosed by his long fingers and his smile followed her as she hastily left the room. When a few minutes later the usual wishes for a happy weekend had been exchanged and her staff had left the office, Miriam clumsily reclined on a chair. Her heartbeat was still more rapid than usual, and it was several minutes before she eventually calmed down.

A bit later she left the office and, shivering, got into her car. Her fingers drummed incessantly on the steering wheel as she fought her way through the weekend traffic. After an endless half-hour she turned into the driveway of her house. Relieved, she noticed Robert's car. Hastening her steps, she ran up the stairs and unlocked the door.

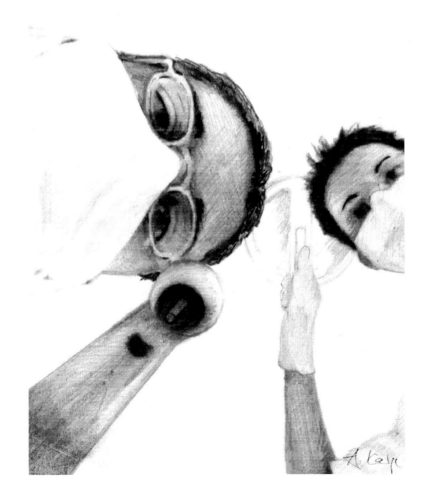

Seconds later she pressed her face against Robert's neck and let her tears flow, while he rocked her in his arms and stroked her hair, as one might a small child. He gently took her face into his hands and, worried, looked at her.

"What's the matter with you, darling? Why, you are trembling. Come, we'll sit down."

Unresisting, Miriam let him lead her to the couch. She fought against her tears and groped for words.

"Oh Robert, it's terrible. Today a new patient came into the practice." Softly she added, "I recognized him right away."

"What do you mean you 'recognized him right away'? Who is he?"

Miriam once more pressed her moist face against the familiar hollow of his neck and haltingly whispered "Winterstein is the man who destroyed my family. He is responsible for what happened to my mother."

A moment of dead silence set in. Robert was suddenly motionless and Miriam sensed that he was holding his breath.

"What are you saying there?" he stammered.

Gently she extracted herself from his embrace and sat up very straight. Her eyes were trying to look into his. "It's exactly as I told you. When you and I met, I told you that my mother had died when I was fifteen years old."

"Sure, but I can't see ..." Robert replied. A thin crease had formed across his forehead.

"You'll understand right away." With a loving gesture she stroked his hand.

"At one time we were a happy family, dad, mom, Felix and me. Of course dad didn't have much time for us because he was so preoccupied with his business. But we were still happy. At least I was, and Felix, too, I think. Mother less so, it seems. And there came a time when we were increasingly aware that our parents were quarreling. But all of a sudden matters seemed to improve again, and they scarcely fought anymore. Then it happened."

Miriam sighed. "It was a Sunday in April. Felix and I had gone down to the basement to play ping-pong. A little while later mom joined us and said that she could no longer endure pretending and had to make a clean breast of things. There was another man in her life, she intended to move in with him, and dad knew it already." A sad smile played around Miriam's lips.

She lowered her gaze and continued in a soft voice: "A week later mom did indeed move out. While dad was at work and Felix at school, she packed two suitcases. I was home from school sick that day and was totally aware of everything. After packing, she talked to someone on the phone, then came into my room and sat on the edge of my bed. She said that she loved Felix and me very much. We were hugging each other, and both of us bawled. When the doorbell rang, she got up and left. She simply went away."

Bewilderment vibrated in Miriam's voice.

"I heard voices downstairs. I jumped out of bed and ran down the stairs. She was still there. A man stood at her side. Younger than dad, with curly hair and deep dark eyes. He was about mom's age. We stared at each other. He didn't say a word, took her suitcases and walked toward the door. I sat down on the lowest step and couldn't stop crying. It was terrible." Miriam swallowed. "And the more I cried the more my hatred grew against this man with the blond curls who had taken our mother away and with that had destroyed our family. At that time I didn't know his name, but a short time later I learned it."

Miriam drew in a deep breath and quickly expelled it again. Enunciating it very carefully, she uttered his name. "Winterstein. I learned his first name only today: Albert. Whenever mom mentioned him, she always spoke of him as Al. Al Winterstein."

Robert bent over and reached for the bottle of juice on the table in front of him. He filled his glass and with a question in his eyes, held it out to Miriam. She shook her head, so he drank a swallow.

"And you are quite sure it was he who came to your office today?"

Miriam nodded. "Absolutely certain. I know that almost thirty years have passed. But it isn't just the same name. His appearance is so unmistakable. The dark brown eyes and the curly blond hair which, of course, has turned almost gray. Then that lean, very tall figure. It's him. One hundred percent."

Pensively Robert let his glance come to rest on her as he posed his next question.

"You once told me that your mother died in a traffic accident. That isn't the case?"

"Yes, Robert, that's true, but it's not accurate that a drunken driver cut in front of her when she had the right-of-way. It was she who was drunk. Drunk and full of sedatives. She herself caused the accident, and, in fact intentionally."

Robert stared at her: "Are you saying that …"

"Yes, Robert." The words were uttered with great bitterness.

"That's the way she committed suicide, and Winterstein drove her to it."

"Why do you believe that?"

"I know it. I know that mom became unhappy after a very short time. She suffered so much being separated from Felix and me, and in addition …" She hesitated for a moment before she hissed, "that shameless swine cheated openly on her. She hinted at it time and again. Dad forbade us to have any contact with her, but several times we met in secret. She looked bad and was visibly losing weight. But she couldn't cut loose from that guy."

Robert looked at her with a sad expression. "Why do you tell me all this only now? Do you have so little trust in me?"

Miriam reached for his hand and gently placed it for a moment against her cheek before pressing a kiss on his slender fingers.

"But Robert, how can you even think something like that. Of course I trust you; otherwise I couldn't have told you all this. We've only known each other for two years. Surely there are things that we don't know about each other yet. There's been no need to tell you all this in detail. It isn't as if I had to think about it constantly. For all intents and purposes I have hardly thought about this story at all. Until this afternoon."

Robert appeared reassured. "Did you see this fellow Winterstein only that one time, the one you told me about?"

"No, the following year I saw him again. I would meet mom in a café, and he would come to pick her up. One time he even sat down with us and ordered tea. He scarcely talked to us, and mom acted quite awkward."

"Do you think that he recognized you today, too?"

"Out of the question. At that time I was an adolescent, a roly-poly girl with long blond pigtails. My hair is much darker now, I wear glasses, have a different family name, and on top of all this, almost thirty years have passed."

"He certainly must have noticed that something wasn't quite right with you. How agitated you were when you came home! I assume you felt the same way in the office … And after him you still treated other patients? You sure have strong nerves!"

"No, he was the last patient. And I believe I was quite controlled. I really became weak-kneed only when everybody had left and I was alone in the office."

Robert got up and buried his hands in his pants pockets. Tensely he walked up and down the room.

"And? Is he coming back one more time? And if so, what happens next?"

Miriam reached for a cigarette.

"To be honest – I don't exactly know. He has an appointment for next week. I'm confident I can treat him quite normally, I will hide my feelings and he'll never return. I still have time in the next few days to prepare for our meeting. It'll work out one way or another."

"Let him have it by giving him amalgam," Robert broke out in a brief and bitter laughter. "You won't be doing him a favor with that. At least that's what some of the experts claim! Oh, Miriam." He sat down next to her once more and pulled her gently into his arms. "My poor sweetheart. I'll always be at your side."

Miriam gratefully pressed close to him. "I'm so glad that I told you all this. I feel better already. Hold me tight Robert, hold me tight …"

On the following Sunday evening Miriam sat by herself in front of the TV. Robert had gone to play tennis with a colleague from work. She was finding it more and more difficult to concentrate on the action, so she turned off the TV and, lost in thought, sipped a glass of red wine. She reflected once again upon all that had happened in the distant past and felt bitterness and rage rising up in her. "I have to be crazy!" crossed her mind. "I find that guy right under my nose; he has practically been delivered into my hands. Why, for heaven's sake, should I let this chance escape me? I never expected to see him again. After all, Berlin isn't a village. Surely it can't be an accident that he landed in my office of all places. What should I do? What did Robert say? I should give him amalgam. Prankster! I'd prefer to give that swine something quite different!"

Miriam had lit a cigarette and refilled her wine glass when an outrageous thought suddenly occurred to her. What had happened, she reflected, while she was still a student? Now she remembered. It had occurred in the department of physiology at the university clinic. Her friend Amy was still working there. The professor had demonstrated to the class the toxic effects of cyanide on cells. Even a tiny quantity sufficed to poison someone, and no one could, of course, prove the presence of the substance. That is, in theory one would be able to, but who would hit on the idea that … ? How would it be, for example, if the substance beneath the filling contained cyanide? How would that affect the patient? And what if the filling were not put in properly? What could happen then?

Miriam sat completely upright at the outermost corner of her sofa and felt her heart was beating faster and faster as she gave free rein to her fantasy.

On the one hand the amalgam filling had to be badly inserted; on the other hand it had to hold for a certain time. At some point, a piece of the filling breaks off, freeing the cyanide. He swallows it; it is absorbed in the small intestine and gets into the bloodstream, then into the individual cell, where it inhibits oxygen intake. The result would be a nice internal suffocation. Winterstein simply collapses, squirms, holds his stomach and – is dead.

Yes, that could work. In addition he had indicated on his medical record that he'd had a heart attack once before.

Given his previous medical history, nobody should suspect that things weren't quite right. What else did he mention? That he was going to America for an extended period. It couldn't be any better, could it?

Quite determined now, Miriam put down her glass and extinguished her half-smoked cigarette in the ashtray. She resolved to look in again on her friend Amy in her laboratory. Probably as soon as tomorrow, right after work. She had done so before from time to time. But this time … A good thing that Amy was so scatterbrained and everything in her lab was lying around unattended.

Miriam breathed deeply and put on a winning smile as she entered the treatment room where Winterstein was already seated.

"Good afternoon, Doctor."

Again his bony hand stretched out to her. She took hold of it with a light shudder. His dark eyes looked at her in an open and friendly manner.

"Good afternoon, Mr. Winterstein. That last filling is due today. Oh, Irene," she turned toward her assistant. "We have so much work; I'll take care of the filling myself. Please go into Room 2 to Mrs. Bremer and polish her new fillings."

Now they were alone, and Miriam felt herself becoming utterly calm. Winterstein opened his mouth, and she began her work. The noise of the air turbine drill intermingled with that of the saliva extractor. "Now comes the lining," she said while she thought *if you only knew*. Then she inserted the new filling. "Well, that's it, Mr. Winterstein. Today is Wednesday. Could you come Monday morning for the polishing?"

He rinsed his mouth and smiling, shook his head. "If possible, I'd prefer tomorrow or Friday. I'm no longer in Berlin on Monday. On Sunday I'm flying to the US."

"Ah yes." Miriam tried to make her voice sound casual. "You mentioned that."

"Yes, now I can indulge in traveling since I retired a short while ago. I'm flying for a few months to visit my brother in Chicago. He emigrated twenty years ago." Winterstein got up from the dental chair.

"Have a good time over there. Till the next time, Mr. Winterstein." *There won't be a next time*, Miriam added mentally, *for soon, Winterstein, you'll be dead.*

"Good bye, Doctor, and thank you very much."

As his hand gripped the doorknob, he turned toward Miriam. "By the way, how is it possible that I have such bad teeth and my brother has such good ones? We are identical twins, you see, and Alfred doesn't have a single filling."

Miriam stared at Winterstein. Her eyes widened in consternation, while in her mind she saw a double edition of Winterstein: Albert and Alfred. Which one was Al Winterstein? She staggered, and her hand, seeking support, clung to the filling table. Winterstein's next words reached her muffled and distant.

"Just imagine that. Actually we should have identical good or bad teeth, shouldn't we?" Miriam fainted, but not before she registered the startled look on Winterstein's face.

"Oh good God, what is the matter with you, Doctor? Please say something!"

His shouting caught Irene's attention just as she was entering the treatment room. Winterstein knelt helplessly at Miriam's side.

"Call a physician, quickly. Your boss has passed out. Seems to have a circulatory problem, poor woman."

The Woman of His Dreams

Britta was the ultimate woman of his dreams. Each time he thought of her – and that happened frequently – something like lightning flashed through him, and a warm tingle flowed through his body.

In vain Peter tried to concentrate on his work. His report had to be submitted within two days. Despite the pressure of time Peter was unable to prevent his thoughts from wandering. Nothing helped. As so often in the past, he would have to work overtime. He sighed while smiling and permitted himself one more daydream, before turning back to his papers with the utmost discipline he could command.

Britta was a splendid woman, and Peter had the feeling that she was quite aware of this. A curly, reddish-brown mane swirled around her narrow face. Her green eyes flashed from beneath long, thick eyelashes. Her eyebrows, reminding Peter of the dark color of honeydew, were constantly in motion like the wings of a bird, undecided where to land. Her narrow nose was covered with saucy freckles. Britta had a mouth with full sparkling lips, shaped for kissing, and when she showed her immaculate teeth while smiling, Peter had to control the impulse to draw her close. She was tall, slender, and with curves in the right places. Her perfume was subtle and intense at the same time, wafting around her elegant body like a transparent cloak.

When Peter saw her for the first time nine years ago, she literally took his breath away, and he instantly felt that he loved this woman and would love her eternally. At the time, he noticed with dismay that a simple wedding ring disfigured the ring finger of her left hand. That immediately threw him into deepest despair. He scarcely heard what she was saying and only regained his composure when she smilingly extended her beringed hand to him. Feeling her cool slender fingers was almost too much for Peter. He held her hand a moment longer than proper and pressed it tenderly. Surprised and irritated at the same time, she withdrew her hand from him and then, smiling, turned to the others.

Peter's glances followed her, and he gave himself over entirely to the pain of his fantasy. He imagined how she wrapped her arms around the neck of a handsome man – her husband – who pulled her girlish figure to himself with a possessive gesture. He imagined her closing those beautiful green eyes during a kiss while the man thrust his hands into her superb head of hair.

"Mr. Schmitz?" Her soft voice put an end to his painful thoughts.

"Yes, yes, of course," Peter answered distractedly. His gaze travelled to her bare forearms. He had never seen forearms as perfect as hers. Her veins were outlined beneath alabaster-colored skin. Not blue, as with him or other ordinary people, but turquoise-colored like a delicate painting on an expensive canvas.

More than anything Peter wished he could see Britta by herself without all those people surrounding her. He imagined how he would reach for her hand, devoid of rings this time, and pull it to his lips. As he did this, he would not lose sight of her face for even a second, and the love, lighting up her emerald-colored eyes, would be meant for him alone.

Reality was different. In these nine years he had encountered her exactly five times. Each time he looked feverishly forward to seeing her again, and for several nights before their meeting he was scarcely able to sleep. When he finally caught sight of her, shook her hand, and spoke to her, he had to acknowledge with distress that she took only a professional interest in him. Her friendliness was somehow noncommittal; he could not take pride in her words, since they were meant just as much for the others as for him.

In her presence Peter was bashful. How gladly he would have exchanged a few words with her privately, paid her a compliment and invited her to have a meal with him. But when he saw her, the wedding ring, and the other people, his courage abandoned him and he cursed his shyness. He feared nothing more than being rejected.

Feeling hurt and helpless he watched how relaxed Christopher was as he talked with Britta. Christopher was not only his colleague, but also a good friend. Despite this, Peter did not dare to confide this unhappy love to him. Although he was not half as good-looking as Peter, Christopher was far more self-confident and courageous. For almost three years now he had been dating Klara and was happy with her. They wanted to get married soon. Peter was to be their witness and had postponed his vacation for just that reason.

As the date approached when Peter was again going to see the woman of his dreams, he was becoming more and more nervous. The last time he had seen her was a year and a half ago and the time had seemed interminable to him. This time he felt everything would be different. It was like a premonition. Something would happen. Something wonderful.

Peter could scarcely await the day. His nervousness increased hour by hour. How would she look? Would she have changed? No. Time seemed to pass this woman by without leaving a trace.

As he was knotting his tie on the morning that held such significance for him, he cast a last glance into the mirror and was satisfied with his appearance: tall, muscular, with thick blond hair and warm brown eyes behind gold-framed eyeglasses. The dental crowns had been a good investment, and the penny-size birthmark on his left cheek lent a peculiar charm to his attractive face. Peter was well received by women, even though it was never he who took the initiative. Women approached him and were charmed by his shyness, which contrasted sharply with his appearance, and they took pleasure in making a conquest of him.

One hour later the time had come. Britta was already there as he entered the room and, as usual, his breathing stopped as he gazed at her. Her hair was somewhat shorter, and she had lost weight. And then he saw it: he could scarcely believe it and with a second glance made sure that he had not been mistaken.

She no longer wore a wedding ring.

Her left hand was completely bare. Only a faint glow on her finger gave a hint that a ring had been in place there until recently. To Peter, Britta appeared more beautiful than ever. Today, this he now knew for sure, today he would ask her, even chancing the danger of having a heart-attack from sheer excitement, or still worse, being rebuffed. He would wait until everything was over and then arrange matters in such a way that he could talk with her alone. It simply had to work. Peter had the feeling that Britta was looking at him differently than in the past, but he was not sure that his imagination was not playing tricks on him.

This time she first exchanged a few words with Christopher before she came up to him and, smiling, extended her hand. Peter gathered every bit of his courage.

"Mrs. Engelhardt," he said in a choking voice, while holding her hand firmly. "When everything is over here, would you have a moment for me?"

So now he had come out with it. Now there was no longer any backing off, and Peter hardly dared to lift his eyes.

"Yes, Mr. Schmitz. Simply remain here afterwards."

Peter wanted to say something, but he managed only a helpless smile. He felt choked with emotion. Twenty minutes later the others left the room little by little. At the door Christopher turned around and looked inquiringly at Peter.

"Are you coming?"

"One moment, Christopher. I'm coming right away."

Peter's throat was dry, and he watched Britta close her fountain pen and shut the document folder. Then she looked at him, smiling.

"Mrs. Engelhardt," Peter gasped and swallowed. "Can I, I mean, would you ..." Peter faltered and ran his tongue across his dry lips. "Mrs. Engelhardt." Peter advanced one step toward her and with an almost daredevil gesture, quite strange for him, he reached for her hand. "May I take you out for dinner?"

Britta Engelhardt looked at him thoughtfully, and was amused at the same time. Her hand still rested in his, and she did not withdraw it.

"Mr. Schmitz, how often have we seen each other?" She smiled.

"Today is the sixth time in nine years," Peter answered. "But today everything is different."

"You are right," said the beautiful justice of peace. "Today, for once, you were the witness and not the bridegroom. What would you do in my position? You are, like

King Bluebeard, a serial groom," she said in a playfully strict voice. "I am the one who should know; after all it was I who married you off five times."

"You're right," Peter sighed, "but I only did it because ..."
He stopped and searched for the right words.

"You don't have to explain anything to me," Britta smiled. "I understand. And I accept your invitation." She hesitated. "And as far as everything else is concerned – give me a bit of time."

Peter's beaming smile seemed to illuminate the room. "I have been waiting for nine years now," he whispered happily, "I am certainly able to wait a bit longer."

Maria

"… but if thou would speak just one word, my soul would heal."

God will not speak to this Maria. The hard wood of the church bench hurts her knees. Perhaps it doesn't hurt enough. But perhaps twenty minutes more will command God's attention. Maria tries to pray, but she can't remember a single prayer, even though as a child she was allowed to attend services at least twice a week. Yes, she was allowed to, because at that time she was a member of the Girl Scouts. Everything was only a game – a beautiful, festive game, which she played with many other kids, and which kept her from wandering in the streets. It was a state-supported, almost free-of-charge babysitter service.

The game stopped when the black-haired fingers of the drunken curate pushed themselves beneath her flimsy, short summer skirt, exploring like fat maggots, separating the not yet bristly down. They thrust themselves single-mindedly, with the fattest maggot leading, into the warm, rosy opening, from which some day the darling little babies were supposed to come, but never came.

"Help me God, please help me!"

Maria can't remember the text from the divine service. For forty years she has not served God in the company of other worshippers. Just a few years ago she called it quits and took the ultimate step. Now she has it in black and white that she appeared in municipal court and declared her separation from the Roman Catholic Church.

Stamped, sealed, and delivered.

Secretly she still goes into churches, but they have to be empty. On these occasions, she sits down on the last bench and recites the Lord's Prayer over and over again. That one she still knows. Sometimes she stares for the longest time at a painted Christ-figure, until her eyes begin to tear and she can't see clearly anymore. Then, for a few seconds, she has the impression that the wooden figure, understanding her fully, is blinking back at her.

Surely it is different to be praying in a large church than at home in front of her household altar. Perhaps she no longer has the right, since her 'disaffiliation', to seek God's help in a church. She sneaks into and out of churches as though she were doing something illegal. She has a guilty conscience, because she herself is bad and fit for nothing. Without a family, without words, without hope.

Maria constantly feels herself tormented by something or someone. This she has learned from her father. Sitting on her piano, serving as repository only for photographs, shells, and papers, and from which she elicits sounds no more than two hours a year perhaps, there is a child's picture in a silver frame. It shows her as a four-year old: a delicate, dark-haired little girl, looking a little worried, but laughing nonetheless. Maria loves and hates that picture at one and the same time because it evokes such powerful feelings in her, and of that she is afraid. It is better to feel nothing, because then one can't be hurt.

The piano stands on one side of the corridor leading to the living room. The little girl in the picture looks at her differently each time. Sometimes full of pity, at other times reproachfully.

It is incomprehensible how one can beat so harshly while confronted by such innocence and endearing charm. What demon is driving her father's fist to pound that white, tender child's flesh and sometimes also to kick it, until the child dissolves in pain and deathly fear? Perhaps there is some secret that Maria has never been able to figure out? To offer no defense and to play dead? Perhaps that would have lessened her suffering, and her father would not have been goaded on by her desperate resistance and pained outcries.

But Maria always screamed when she was being mistreated, though she must have had an intuition that her father really hated to beat her. He simply couldn't help himself. His fate was an illness that had reduced him to being one of the youngest retirees in the country. He wanted so much to be able to earn a living for his wife and daughter by his own hard work, but after being told he would not live much longer, he had transferred all his rage and frustration into a pair of hands condemned to idleness, and had given them the task, albeit a senseless one, of beating his offspring.

Maria had loved her father more than anyone on earth. Because for as long as he lived he confronted her with a challenge, to struggle for his respect and love. She never had to engage in that with her mother. She was certain of her mother's love as well as her inability to protect her only child. It was the mother who had to earn money in order to feed the small family – the child with the sad eyes and the sick husband. The shocking discovery of his illness, barely nine months after the wedding, sent the pregnant mother into premature labor. His generally anticipated death would probably make her a young widow. That was also the reason for denying themselves a second child. A widow with one child can manage better than one with two. In the meantime, it was the father's task, till his death, to take care of preparing the main meal each day. For this his hands were well equipped; almost everything he cooked tasted good.

How much Maria would have liked to have had a child – a clone of herself. A new, small Maria, who could be compensated for the sins that had been visited upon the old, mature Maria. To see oneself grow up, beloved, cared for, protected. The world would be wide open for the new Maria, with all the abilities and talents which had been lying fallow for so long within the old Maria.

Maria harbored these and similar abstruse dreams at night, when she really should have been sleeping and resting up from doing nothing. But sleep abandoned her when she was still a small, slim child, four or five years old, sleeping in a wooden bed with metal bars at the foot of her parents' bed in that tiny two-room apartment. One night, awakened suddenly by strange noises, she finds the bed of her parents empty. Frightened, her heart beating fast, she climbs out of her tiny bed, opens the door to the other room, the living room-kitchen, and stares in horror at the scene that confronts her already permanently sad eyes. Her father is kneeling on the floor, vomiting blood into a large, white enamel pail, her mother next to him, holding him, with nothing to hold onto herself. And without a telephone. Go back to bed, go on, go. But the child can't go. She can't move out of fear and fascination at the same time. Her mother gets up, rushes out to get help. She runs a long distance, far, no sense waking the neighbors; they too have no telephone.

Maria's father turns his ashen face toward the child. Do go to bed, he says, before a fresh red torrent gushes from his mouth. The child is trembling so much that her teeth are chattering. She does not dare go to her father to hold him as her mother had done. It's better not to get close to him now. Who knows? Who knows, perhaps he'll get furious. The child must be on her guard, always on her guard; you never know.

Her mother returns, runs nervously back and forth between the bleeding man and the door; then the deliverance of the ringing doorbell. The ambulance has arrived. She is supposed to come along to the hospital; her husband will probably not last the night. It's his fifth and most serious hemorrhage in the past four years. Eventually the end inevitably comes – then prayers no longer help and even very young retirees must die.

The child, where to take the child. While the man is being bedded down on a stretcher, the woman brings the child to bed, covers her up, strokes her cheek, and tells her she can go back to sleep now and not to be afraid. Everything will turn out all right and mommy will come back as soon as possible. Then there is complete silence.

The child lies in her tiny bed and strains her ears. Her whole body is tense, and she scarcely dares to breathe, so that she cannot fail to detect any noise or movement. Several times sleep is about to overtake her, but the child's willpower is stronger, she fights back and struggles back to wakefulness; anything but falling asleep – who knows what might happen then. Something horrible might happen if she falls asleep, so she must stay awake. And she stays awake the whole night. Then she hears the key turn in the lock; that's the noise she has been waiting for; her mother comes to the child directly; her father is still alive, but for how long? The bitter cup of being half-orphan has not yet passed. Now waiting and praying again is what must be done.

Since that time Maria has forgotten how to sleep. She is known as the woman who does not sleep, whom one can phone at any time, even in the dead of night, she, who is still listening intensely, fighting sleep, desperately waiting.

Maria has told this time and again, including to the physicians in the clinics, this and all the terrible experiences that had prevented her from feeling carefree as a child. Life is hard, if one is born not a child but a grownup who drinks responsibility with every swallow of her mother's milk.

Maria is waiting for life to begin at last. Isn't it time now, at the beginning of her fifties? Until now, she has not lived, only survived. She wants to look ahead because what lies ahead can only be better than what lies behind. But the past does not let her go. The deepest hurts are the father-wounds, and the constant memories are the salt that prevents them from healing. Remembering is something concrete. With it you know what you own. For Maria, looking forward means to dream of better times, of salvation, and of the life that she surely deserves, after all. The most difficult challenge to endure is the present. She does not know what to do with the present; it is the unavoidable connecting link between the remembered and the hoped-for, but it is insubstantial and without structure.

Maria rejoices over every day that she has put behind her. She is frequently surprised by the fact that she is still alive. Since childhood, she has told everyone that she won't get old. That, too, she has inherited from the words of her father. No matter what came up – it was all the same to him, since he wouldn't get old anyway. In that case, why expend effort, learn something, strain oneself? He lived to be fifty-eight years old, cheated an early, often wished-for death, given the consolation of the Holy Roman Church, and tumbled into the kingdom of Hell. He sits at the right hand of his father, a still greater tyrant, and bemoans his misspent life.

Every day Maria goes for a walk. Always the same stretch across fields, a path along the forest, then through the industrial area and home or the same route in reverse. A paved street divides the landscape like a straightened grey river. The walk takes from sixty to eighty minutes, depending on whether Maria keeps her head up and walks with sprightly steps or, deep in tortuous thoughts, examines the ground. Events on the ground are often more interesting than those at eye level. There it is important to avoid stepping on ants, caterpillars, and snails, to help overturned bugs get back on their feet, to register the motley colors of the plants and the garbage at the side of the road, to be happy about the former and annoyed about the latter, to hear the twittering of birds, the hammering of woodpeckers, and the barking of dogs, who provide human beings some outdoor exercise. One can count the flattened residues of chewing gum and try to imagine the jaws that kept grinding them, also watch out for puddles during a rain and walk around them, because none of Maria's shoes are waterproof. For that reason, she keeps a supply of thin plastic bags, which she gets at the supermarket's fruit and vegetable department and which she slips on and fastens around the tops of her stockings before going for a walk in the rain.

It takes willpower for Maria to undertake that walk every day, but she has two reasons for steeling herself anew for it. One is the satisfaction she feels when she returns home. At least in that respect she succeeds half-way in her self-discipline. The other reason is the more important one, even if it sounds banal. Maria fights for her health, or rather against her illnesses, some of which have plagued her ever since childhood. An almost inevitable development, when everything revolves around this topic in the parental home. Even though her ill father had rarely broached the subject, it tragically changed the behavior of her mother. She constantly talked about illnesses or methods of staying healthy. Relevant articles were clipped from newspapers, or TV programs about illnesses or good health were watched. Thick volumes dealing with health decorated the living room cupboard and lent it, at least from a distance, an intellectual ambiance. The aromas of Franciscan brandy, chamomile tea, and cod-liver oil hovered, alternately, over everything.

Maria was unable to divest herself of that atmosphere, not even after she had left her parents' house. Defiantly she has smoked now for more than thirty years. She simply can't let go of that vice.

When Christian entered her life, illness and death were suddenly relegated to a subordinate role. The yen for life, the longing for happiness and fulfillment reigned supreme. When the relationship ended, the old thoughts and anxieties returned, stronger than before.

Maria has been divorced now for more than twenty years. From that time until her ex-husband's fatal accident four years ago, he never learned that a kiss was Maria's real reason for separating from him after a brief marriage. A passionate, wild kiss during a party, with which a small Venezuelan, ten years younger, had at first overwhelmed, then challenged her. The kissing duel had lasted for nearly one hour and had ended in a tie.

She arrived home with glowing lips and with the realization, already dimly perceived during her return, that she now had to separate from Christian despite her love for him. She was thankful that her husband, as usual, would not be home until the weekend, and that she would not have to explain her state of mind immediately.

Christian was a dear, nice bore, reliable, terribly anxious to be on the safe side, who relished his sweet wife on weekends and glossy porno magazines during the week. Sometime in the future he would amount to something, and then one would be able to afford a little house with a garden, also two children, a stylish car, and an annual vacation. A savings account, which he had opened at the beginning of his professional training, would help to realize these ambitions.

Maria had fallen in love with Christian because he was so handsome. She had immediately fallen in love with him; after all, he looked as if he had stepped out of one of her favorite pictures, a happy Amor victorious, as Caravaggio had once immortalized him. Maria, for her part, had been told by an art history student that she resembled Mademoiselle Lanthelme as portrayed in a painting by Boldini, so that she and Christian were a classic example of a truly beautiful couple. During their first months together, Maria worshipped Christian and suffered severe pangs of jealousy, a feeling previously alien to her. She viewed them as a measure of her love for him. At that time she had threatened to leave him immediately if he should so much as kiss another woman. The image of him kissing another woman was unbearable for her, a kiss perhaps as an overture – she did not want to go even that far in her thoughts. And now it had happened to her. Her kiss-smothered lips were burning, and she had to act now. She could not use different yardsticks. It was not Christian who had kissed a stranger and therefore had to be abandoned, but she who had done it and now she must leave. When she confronted her husband the next time they met, she gave the months-long tensions between them as the reason for her decision. Those really did exist, but Maria embellished, exaggerated, grew more and more intense, wept, gave up, and finally began to believe that it was hopeless herself and that their marriage had to end.

Resentments that had smoldered but had long been suppressed erupted all at once into unavoidable, love-destroying differences. Fascinated, Maria heard herself arguing, sobbing, and coming to a decision. She did not give her husband a chance; she let everything spill out in order to come to a conclusion, but she steered clear of clarifying anything and left him in her backwash, desperate and helpless.

It was impossible for her to confess that kiss. A kiss of that duration could not be forgiven. She could not forgive herself. She now had to punish herself and get out, leave behind that good middle-class nest and husband, who was perhaps not the right one, but who certainly had been the most handsome. She had to plunge a dagger into a heart which had beaten only for her.

Some people judged Maria's refusal of alimony as stupid, others as decent. Nobody knew that it was nothing more than a legal expression of a guilty conscience; nobody knew, not even the little Venezuelan, whom Maria never saw again, even though, as she learned later, he had inquired several times about her.

Maria had anticipated an early death when she was scarcely twenty years old, and this thought had induced her at that tender age to compose a will, other versions of which were to follow at a later time. Without the stamp of a notary public. Simply for herself. Handwritten in royal blue ink, it began with the words: "In full possession of my mental powers," and it ended with the instruction that she wished to be cremated and the urn buried at the cemetery in G.

Maria deluded herself into thinking that she was rich. After all, she had been given a piano by her parents at first communion; four thousand marks had accumulated in her savings account by that time; she possessed a solid gold chain, which her maternal grandmother had bequeathed to her. In addition, her childless uncle, who was also her godfather, had given her a small car for her high-school graduation. It was a used car, but you don't look a gift horse in the mouth nor in the opposite end either.

According to Maria's will, her mother was to get the piano, and her father a thousand marks to lose at his much-beloved dog races. The boy who had deflowered her shortly before high-school graduation and who had displayed a great deal of sensitivity by day and night was to get her car. The gold chain was willed to her best girl friend, the only one she had ever had and who, just three years after Maria drafted the will, died miserably of leukemia. Three thousand marks remained for SOS-Children's Village, Green Peace, and Amnesty International.

Maria was satisfied. Come what may, she had now put her affairs in order. What came was life and not death. For that Maria felt less well prepared.

After her separation from Christian, a second marriage appeared to her completely unrealistic. Why should she tie herself down to a man once more and possibly have children, if they would have to become semi-orphans at an early age? To start a family clearly was not the way to go.

For the first time in her fifty years, she became conscious of the fact that she had imitated her father in her conduct and how, also just like him, she had for the most part avoided life's responsibilities. Maria's life had consisted of taking care of her numerous physical complaints and of being available to her parents. It was easy to push aside all responsibilities if an early demise was lying in wait.

In the year since she turned fifty, a change had taken place in her inner makeup. For so long she had scarcely missed an opportunity to point out that she would not grow old, believing an early death to hover over her like a tragic knell of fate, as it had done years ago over her father. But in the course of the years something had imperceptibly happened that Maria had not counted on: she had grown older. Unbelieving and with a mixture of astonishment and euphoria, Maria had awakened on the morning of her fiftieth birthday and had recalled that by her own prognostication, she should have been dwelling below ground for several years already. Now she had to face the fact that she couldn't rely on her own predictions. What could she conclude from that? How would it be if she had also erred about other aspects of her life? What if not only a long life lay before her, but perhaps also working in a profession? Or even finding a life companion?

Maria scarcely dared to follow that thought to its conclusion. This positive development had not begun immediately on her fiftieth birthday. No. It was a mental game of Box and Cox. The initial euphoria was followed by a feeling of having been cheated. She had never reckoned on getting this old and this is what she had also told all of her acquaintances. Had she now lost her credibility? Would it now annoy people that she still remained among them, having simply grown older in the meantime?

Her acquaintances know very little about Maria; of course, the salient facts of her life, that she is divorced and out of work and has health problems, certainly. But otherwise she follows an aria by Franz Lehar: always keep smiling and always be good-humored … She rarely speaks about subjects that depress and frighten her, not even with her mother. That was quite different in earlier years, but with her increasing age she had developed a need to reveal little, to settle things in her own mind and to answer questions about her well-being with "good." Maria's mother will not live forever, after all, so it makes sense to cut the umbilical cord in time. Besides, she has her own little altar at home, in addition to the churches that she still enters surreptitiously time after time. The medium-sized picture of Christ, which once belonged to Christian's grandmother, she was allowed to keep after the divorce. On the small table below it, there were candles, incense sticks and an aromatic oil lamp, dried flowers and a rosary. During her times of infinite sadness and hopelessness, she seeks asylum in prayer and fervently asks for help. Since it has become clear to her that God hadn't planned to take her into His fold at a young age, she is trying to adjust to life and more and more frequently, if hesitantly, to forge plans for the future. Amazed, she notices that the past no longer assumes the major role in her life and that her forward-looking thoughts are becoming more and more concrete and realistic. Little by little she deals differently with her physical complaints. She does not drive herself crazy anymore and is more composed. What might be the reason for all this? Perhaps because she is now approaching the change of life. Change of life. A neat phrase. A life change, exchanging something. A curious word, if one does not place it in some sort of context. To change, exchange, interchange.

Deep inside, Maria feels more strongly prepared for change and is in suspense about what will happen to her. And it is clear to her that she herself must do something about it.

While taking a walk, Maria comes to a decision. Something must happen in her life. Things can't go on like this. She decides to get married within a year. Getting a job would do as well, but for that she is too old. "Money or sex" resounds through her head, and she has to laugh as she remembers an episode that happened when she was in her early twenties. She had to run an errand in town, and she needed to choose which way to go: either a parking lot rather far out on the edge of town and then a fifteen-minute walk, or a parking lot directly behind the railroad station, separated from the inner city only by a dark underpass. As she approached the underpass, she caught sight of four dubious figures who had found a cozy place on a small wall directly in front of the steps. Beer bottles and raucous voices showed that their little party had already been going on for some time. Not a person in sight, near or far. Defiantly, Maria pushed out her chin and with a self-assured stride approached the entrance to the underpass. One man separated himself from the small group and, swinging his beer bottle, walked toward Maria. "Money or sex," he barked at her, while fingering his belt with his free hand. Maria immediately answered: "With your looks, I prefer your money." The man was too drunk to react quickly and by the time he understood the meaning of her words, she had already run past him into the underpass. A short sprint and she had reached safety. His enraged insults and the laughter of his drinking buddies slowly faded away in the long underpass. Well, that had turned out all right. Her father had been utterly delighted by her reaction, and this, it occurs to Maria as she remembers this incident with a bitter taste, had always been finally the most important thing to her.

It is time now for the longed-for change. It is time for Maria to liberate herself from this day-to-day monotony and to finally reward herself with something. Nice trips, a big car, and, above all, a different home: larger, more quietly situated, with a balcony or a garden and with a bathtub. It grates on her nerves that she can only shower. In addition, her landlady, a widowed retired schoolteacher, is too stingy to let her have really hot water. The thermostat in the basement is permanently set at 101 degrees Fahrenheit. That will have to do. Any higher is too expensive. Maria knows all about economizing, but has no tolerance for stinginess. Especially when the landlady's late husband had been an administrative director and had plenty of money.

Different furniture, a new wardrobe, a bit of luxury. A man must be found, who will offer Maria all this, without making demands, a provider. Her contribution in return? She'll have to see. In any case, no sex. She has lost the desire; she is tired, exhausted, and of the opinion that she has seen and felt enough naked men. Of course there are differences, but few surprises, and hardly any of those turn out well. She does not find it particularly exciting to sleep with a man. It disturbs her peace and costs her too much strength. Only rarely does she permit herself to be persuaded rather than convinced, for she finds it hard to say no. This is something she has in common with her cousin Valerie, who counts as her own four children, who could have any of five or six fathers. No exact details are known. Simply family ties. For several hours Maria refines a text until she is satisfied with the draft for an ad.

MARRIAGE WITHOUT SEX
The first half of my life consisted mostly of worries, stress, and misfortune. For the second half, I am looking to share good conversations, culture, nature, peace and quiet with an intelligent, loving gentleman, who will give an exhausted, introspective woman protection and security on the basis of a platonic relationship. You can look forward to a very charming, warm-hearted artist, smart, full of humor, slender and pretty, who is aiming for marriage, supported by genuine friendship and mutual care. Your response with picture will reach me under the following code ...

Maria likes the ad she has written. It implies that she is no longer a particularly young person but does not reveal her precise age. Also, she likes the description "artist," because that is what she really is ... an artist in the art of living.

She plans to allow herself some time with this ad and to find out how much an ad this size will cost to place in the weekend edition of a national newspaper.

Maria is careful with her money, and she does not find it difficult to get along on the small monthly benefit payment she receives from the unemployment office. She pays only a modest amount in rent. She disposed of the little Fiat several years ago; too many repairs, too many expenses. If she has errands to run downtown, she bicycles four kilometers; a large supermarket and a discount store are both very close.

She has obtained an identity card from the unemployment office, which entitles her to attend diverse cultural events without charge. This is hugely important to Maria; it is hard for her to imagine a life without opera and theater. She enjoys going to the opera more in winter than in the summer. On those occasions, she loves to show off her mother's broadtail fur coat, cut narrow with a collar of mink, also soft leather gloves. Below her hat, drawn down deep onto her face, her dark curls spread out, already laced with white streaks. On her delicate feet she wears high-heeled pumps. Everything is in black; the only light features are her face and her well-formed calves. Large golden earrings, an inheritance from her grandmother, round out the image of perfect elegance. When she stands at the ticket window, fishing in her purse for the identity card qualifying her for free admission, a smile plays around her cherry-red-painted lips. She enjoys the glances of the other opera-goers, the evaluating and envious ones of the women and the surreptitious and curious ones of the men who accompany them. She looks at least ten years younger than her age, and she's still the same size as she was thirty years ago.

Only once does she experience a situation which she finds embarrassing. The man from the unemployment office who handles her case, also an opera fan, addresses her in the lobby and pays her a compliment about her appearance before she can deposit the expensive fur coat at the check room. Maria can't truly take pleasure in this, but after all, having to live on unemployment insurance does not mean having to run around in sackcloth and ashes for someone who has, in the past, seen better times.

Other than the cultural events that Maria likes to attend – always alone – she lives quite a secluded life. She has no friends and only a small circle of acquaintances. Because of her cheerful and high-spirited temperament, she is a born solo entertainer; her wit and her intelligence are appreciated by the few people who see her at irregular intervals. Certainly there are some among them who would label Maria their friend, but the reverse is not true. By Maria's definition, friendship implies that the other person occupies an important place in one's own life, that one worries about that person's welfare, talks with him or her about everything, and that he or she is part of a self-selected family. Nothing like that is true of the people with whom Maria occasionally associates. She likes them, but she does not think about them when she is not with them. Inwardly she feels free and without genuinely close ties to anyone – with the exception of two women, of whom one is her mother. Because of her entertainment value, Maria is occasionally invited to parties. Sometimes that leads to a visit to the movies, going for a walk, or a lunch or dinner invitation. No one expects an invitation in return. Everybody knows that Maria has no money. Maria lets them believe this, but she knows better. She has told no one that she always has some piano students, whom she invariably keeps for two years. Some families are sad when she tells them that the learning sessions must end, but she has her principles. She herself had only four years with a rather bad female teacher and, although she gives other reasons for terminating her students' lessons, the fact is she can only maintain her high standards for two years. She saves the money she receives for the piano lessons in a giant cookie jar. The bills, meticulously assembled and carefully flattened, lie safely ensconced within their glimmering gold metallic hiding place.

Chewing peanuts and smoking, Maria is sitting beneath the slanting ceiling of her kitchen and listening attentively to a radio feature about the role of psychiatry in Austria during the first half of the twentieth century, when her telephone rings. She hears a feminine voice record something on the answering machine in the next room. When the feature is over, she will listen to the message and find out who called. No need to hurry.

This has changed as well. Maria no longer feels strongly about being reachable at all times and by everybody. Why should she? After all, she is not registered on a waiting list to receive an organ transplant. She also does not participate in the cell phone craze. It is bad enough to be exposed to the incessant tintinnabulation of other people's phones in public places, not to mention the effects of electromagnetic radiation.

For her mother's sake, Maria has an answering machine, which she acquired right after the death of her father. At first her mother would frequently leave messages and ask, weeping, for a call-back, but now this hardly happens anymore. They have established a three-times-a-week phone call timetable, and each of them is comforted knowing that the other is doing fine. The mother is actually doing far better than her daughter. She is the chair of the Wellness Club in her city, loves traveling, evenings playing bridge, and Sonya. In her old age Maria's mother has found great love once more. Once, during her very early youth, Sonya had a short affair with a man and had a daughter with him. In the fifty years or so since then, Sonya has loved only women. Now in her late-sixties, she has scarcely any contact with her only child, but her grandson Mark visits her regularly. A young computer science student, Mark is, little by little, introducing his grandmother to the secrets of information technology.

Maria's mother and Sonya became acquainted fifteen years ago at the cemetery, where the urns with the remains of Maria's father and those of a female companion of Sonya's, victim of an auto accident, were lying next to one another. The grieving women met every day at the graves, consoled each other, and felt connected to the ashes of their loved ones by keeping their grave stones clean, by igniting the eternal flame, and by arranging the varying flower decorations. Their conversations became more prolonged and increasingly intense and intimate; eventually the meetings at the cemetery began leading to strolls and other activities. Sonya had soon fallen in love with the attractive Elisabeth, but had the good sense to restrain herself. Elisabeth, for her part, tried for a long time to suppress her feelings about the relationship that had existed between her new acquaintance and the accident victim. She liked Sonya, but she could not imagine a sexual relationship at her age even with a man, much less with a woman.

When she finally agreed, a year after her husband's death, to spend a two-week vacation with Sonya in the Black Forest, she gave no thought to the fact that Sonya had reserved a double room for them. That seemed purely practical so that both could save money.

Sonya began using all her wiles to seduce Elisabeth. During the evening they slipped under the cover, turned off the light, and talked for a long while. Sonya had reached out for Elisabeth's hand and was delighted that it was not withdrawn. Even after they had fallen silent, they continued to hold hands. Eventually Elisabeth had slowly removed her hand, murmured "good night" and turned aside. Two nights later, she did not resist Sonya giving her a good-night kiss on her mouth. After a week, they slept arm-in-arm, and by the time they returned home, they were a loving couple.

Elisabeth began to bloom, spoke less and less about illnesses, and was enjoying her belated happiness to the hilt. The two women had succeeded in finding two adjoining apartments in a multi-family apartment building. After her husband's death, Elisabeth had wanted to live alone, but not necessarily in an apartment as large as the one in which she had lived with him during the last six years before his death. In addition, the rent was too high for a single person, and therefore, in the second year of her widowhood she moved into a two-room apartment with a balcony with a view to the southwest beneath the flat roof of the sixth floor. Sonya moved in half a year later, when the apartment next door had become vacant. The two women cooked together, went only now and then to the cemetery, read to one another, and were full of gratitude that they had found each other. When they lay in bed in one apartment or the other, in close embrace, they stroked each other for hours and each whispered tender words to the other. They did not notice the folds and wrinkles, the age-marks and the slack skin, or the bluish veins that wound their way closely beneath their skin that was, in some spots, beginning to resemble parchment. And since they looked upon each other with eyes full of love, they were beautiful; they were not old, but rather experienced, not wilted, but rather mature and happy, so happy …

Maria frequently has to smile when she thinks of her mother and Sonya, her "substitute mother." She recalls the time when she first went to visit her mother in her new apartment in the distant city, and stayed for an entire week. Elisabeth had often told her about Sonya, without revealing their precise relationship. Maria certainly knew about their frequent joint activities and vacations. Mother's best girl friend. What she did not know before became clear to her within minutes when she watched the two women together. They naturally made an effort to be impersonal in their conduct toward each other, but their glances and small gestures gave them away. Maria told them straight out what she thought and they froze. But when they realized that Maria was smiling and apparently did not object to this love, their tension disappeared.

While they were having coffee, Maria sat opposite the two women, both past their best years. They exchanged such loving, intimate glances that Maria couldn't help thanking Sonya for not having turned her mother's head a few decades earlier. Otherwise she would hardly be sitting here. A relieved laughter was the answer, and by then the two lovers had shed their inhibitions about stroking each other's hands in Maria's presence. It annoyed Maria a bit that she had never seen her parents exchanging such tenderness. She was also surprised by a new expression in her mother's eyes. They beamed pure bliss. From this moment on, she had two mothers and after a while, she felt that it had always been this way.

Her substitute mother, Sonya, has left a message, as Maria realizes at the end of the radio feature. This is quite unusual and Maria hopes that nothing has happened to her mother. But no, Sonya's voice sounds thoroughly happy. Could Maria call back? She, Sonya, has a big favor to ask.

Maria dials Sonya's number, and someone lifts the receiver at the other end after the very first ring.

"Schubert here, good evening."

"Hello, Sonya, this is Maria. Is everything all right?"

"Sure, sure, my child."

The corners of Maria's mouth turn upward in amusement. It's strange to be called "my child" by a woman who is only seventeen years older, especially at her age.

"You are probably surprised that I am calling you, but Elisabeth said I shouldn't hesitate to ask you whether something that I have been thinking about is possible. Well, you see, it concerns the following," Sonya continues somewhat laboriously. "I had a call today from my cousin Hildegard. She's been living for the past fifty years in W. She has a son, Valentin. The big trade fair is taking place in your town next week, as you know. So Valentin asked Hildegard whether she knows anyone who lives there. Hildegard remembered my telling her some time ago that you live very close to K. So he's asking whether he can stay with you for a couple of days. As it turns out, he really would only need a place to stay at night, since he will, of course, be at the trade fair during the day. If it wouldn't be any trouble for you … As things stand right now, Valentin hasn't been able to get a hotel room anywhere; he probably didn't take care of it in time. Well, so I thought it doesn't cost anything to ask. And on the subject of cost, he of course wants to pay you for the lodging."

"I don't know right off, Sonya," Maria replies cautiously. She is not accustomed to having visitors and especially not overnight visitors. "Do I have to give you an answer right now or could I sleep on it for a night?"

"Of course you can, my dear."

Maria has to smile again. Sonya is even worse than her mother.

"You see, I so rarely have visitors." She could just as easily have said 'never', but she doesn't.

"Well, there would certainly be room enough …"

She hesitates for another moment, and then she blurts out: "Oh, what's the difference … Okay, let him come." Surprised by her own spontaneous answer, Maria does not say any more and tightens her grip on the receiver.

"Oh, that is really very nice, dearest. Valentin will be very delighted. I'll phone Hildegard first thing tomorrow morning and at the same time give her your address."

"Do you actually know this Valentin?"

"To say I know him would be an exaggeration. I met him twice in W., when I visited Hildegard, but the last time was almost twenty years ago. I don't mean that I haven't visited Hildegard since then, but Valentin wasn't there on those occasions," Sonya explained. "I really can't tell you much about him. I found him likeable and he had decidedly good manners. That much I can still recall. He has been a widower for the last couple of years, and he has a son who is studying in F. I think Valentin has something to do with art, but I can't recall for sure. Hildegard always goes into raptures when she talks about him."

"Okay then, let him come," Maria offers once more, then passes on greetings to her mother and hangs up.

Valentin, a beautiful name, Maria thinks and, smiling, lights up one of her beloved menthol cigarettes. For a long time she remains seated in her candlelit kitchen and enjoys the stillness.

After Maria has said her evening prayer in front of the house altar, she goes to bed, but she does not intend to sleep. She pushes a few pillows behind her back, puts on her reading glasses, and reaches for a fat novel that is lying on her nightstand. A glass of red wine and an ashtray stand next to the lamp. Maria lights another cigarette and opens the book. For a moment she thinks of her mother who would be horrified to see her daughter smoking in bed. Maria chuckles and enjoys the attraction of the forbidden fruit, even though this "fruit" had never been explicitly forbidden. The right kind of concentration eludes her today. Her thoughts constantly wander off and turn to the as yet unknown Valentin. What kind of man might he be? What will he look like? Perhaps he is someone with whom she can have good conversations. Perhaps …

Maria does not notice how her right hand, holding the book, slowly glides down from her drawn-up thighs.

Neither does she notice how the fourth cigarette that she has smoked in bed burns down little by little. Sleep has overcome her. Maria feels its onset, and this time she does not fight it off. She slides down into Morpheus' arms, full of devotion, trust, and hope.

The Evil Child

Sandra was unable to give her mother an explanation for what she had done. Even after Lena had shaken her and slapped her face, Sandra remained silent. Her blond curls cascaded across her face; her gray eyes with their long eyelashes stared at a point far in the distance. Her small mouth quivered, but she pressed her lips tightly together. She had slung her thin arms firmly around herself, as if in this way she could protect herself against everything.

Lena stopped screaming and shaking Sandra. She was only sobbing softly now. Slowly she sank down on her knees in front of her daughter and removed her hands from the girl's narrow shoulders. With an absent-minded gesture she pushed some hair out of her face. Trembling, she wiped the tears from her eyes with a handkerchief.

"All this simply can't be true." Softly and with a hoarse voice she formed her words. "I … I …" she faltered and once more she wiped her reddened eyes with the handkerchief. Lena sought Sandra's eyes, but the child continued staring into the distance.

Her mother crawled the length of the children's room on all fours and finally sat down on the soft carpeted floor, her back leaning against the wall. With tired eyes she looked at her child who had suddenly become so strange to her that she almost could not believe it.

"Sandra … Sandra, why did you do that?!" Lena's voice was scarcely more than a whisper. Breathing heav-

A Kaye

ily she pressed the handkerchief against her chest. Sandra was still standing in the same position, motionless. Suddenly her hand relaxed. She took one backward step in the direction of her bed and sat down on the edge. Slowly she groped for the time-worn stuffed rabbit at the headboard of her bed, pressed it against her chest, and buried her face in its frazzled hide. She still had given no answer to her mother's question.

"My God. How could you ever ..." Lena was searching for the right words. "How can you hug a toy animal in a situation like this? Do you understand at all what you have done?"

Lena's voice was rising. "I simply can't understand it. How could you do something like this? Damn it, now answer me!"

Sandra's silence was becoming oppressive.

Awkwardly Lena got back to her feet and glanced at her wristwatch. "I am going down to Grandma now. You get undressed and go to bed. Tomorrow we are going to bury Daisy in the garden. And then I'll demand an explanation. Is that clear?" She didn't wait for an answer. With slow steps she walked to the door. Her head was throbbing. She felt years older. As she walked out she turned around once more, but Sandra remained sitting on the edge of the bed, her position unchanged.

"Did she say anything?"

With a serious expression Louise looked up as her daughter entered the living room.

"No, Mom. I can't get anything out of her." Lena reached for a few pretzels and sat down opposite her mother. "I've tried everything – scolding, hitting, and kind words, but Sandra simply won't say a single word." She chewed deliberately and stared reflectively at the photograph of Sandra hanging above the living room couch.

"It's absolutely incomprehensible to me. Sandra is otherwise such a dear girl. How could she have been capable of something like that? Do you remember when we gave her Daisy as a Christmas gift three years ago? A guinea pig for a sad little girl. It was the best we could do for her. I think it was the first time she was happy again after Ron's death. Oh Mother ..." Lena sighed. "It's all my fault. If I had had more time for Sandra and Daniel, none of this would have happened. This job uses up all my strength and time. And on top of all that the constant change of shifts. I'll never get used to it. I simply don't have the nerves or the patience for the children. If I didn't have you, Mom, I wouldn't know how I'd manage."

Lena clasped her legs and supported her chin on one of her knees. Helplessly she looked up at her mother. Louise sat upright upon the couch and twisted a curl of her formerly blond hair. With great sympathy she eyed her daughter and sighed deeply.

"All right, all right, calm down." She tried to make her voice sound firm and on the harsh side, but she did not succeed. "You aren't helping anybody when you blame yourself. You're handling things quite well, and the fact that I cook for the children now and then and take care of them, why, that's only natural. First of all I'm their grandma, and secondly, we all live together. And besides, it's good for me and it gives me something to do." She hesitated. "I don't have an explanation for what Sandra did either. It's horrible and utterly incomprehensible. To be honest I could believe this far more easily of Daniel. He's at a difficult age. As it is, I scarcely get to see him face-to-face any more. For all practical purposes he only comes home for lunch and to sleep."

"You're right. But crazy as it sounds, I can't worry about everything. He gets halfway decent grades at school; he doesn't smoke, and the few friends I get to see now and then could be worse. I really don't know that much about him now. Also he never comes to me except when he wants money." Lena once more reached out for some pretzels. "As it is, Ron's absence is noticeable everywhere. It isn't good for children to grow up without their father. And as for me …" She did not finish the sentence and wiped away a tear from the corner of her eye.

Louise groped for her slippers with her feet, slowly rose and smoothed down her skirt. On the way to the door she placed her hands on Lena's shoulder for a moment.

"Tomorrow is another day. Besides it's Sunday. Perhaps we get Sandra to say something tomorrow. I'll go to bed now. Good night, my child."

"Good night, Mom. I'll just make myself a cup of coffee and then I'm going to the clinic. When Daniel comes home … Oh, let it go. He'll get to know about it soon enough. By the way, do you happen to know where he is?"

"No, but where would a sixteen-year-old boy be on a Saturday night?! Good night, or rather I wish you a night with very little hustle and bustle."

"Thank you, Mom. Sleep well."

The door handle was pushed down very slowly and cautiously. Sandra scarcely dared to breathe. Her hands clutched the bed cover so hard that her knuckles turned white. Her heart beat hard and fast, booming in her chest. The moon was shining brightly through the thin cotton drapes, suffusing the room with a cold silvery light. Sandra was able to make out the contours of her brother. Like a shadow Daniel slipped into the room. He pulled the wicker chair within a few feet of her bed before he sat down.

"Well, well, my little sister, have you missed me?" His tone of voice was at once nervous and mocking and kept down to a whisper.

Now Sandra could see him very clearly in the bright moonlight. Everything was exactly as it had been so often in the recent months. Daniel fiddled with his zipper.

"See, today something happened to me again, hard to believe. I told you once about Miss Leonhardt, our new student teacher. A really hot slut. She always wears those tiny miniskirts and tight blouses with a low neckline. Baby, someday her tits will fall out. You know, her tits aren't really that big, but good to grab ahold of …" Daniel laughed goat-like and put his right hand into his pants. "With big hard nipples. And as for her hair! She has long black curls, looks like a gypsy. Well, I gave her three wrong answers today, and then she said I had to stay after class, she wanted to talk to me. She sorted her junk and little by little everybody left the room. And do you know what happened next? You won't believe it. She went to the door, locked it, and then, without any warning, she came up to me. She grabbed me and put her tongue in my mouth. And at the same time she took hold of my balls."

Sandra again heard the noise that she hated so much and filled her with fear, the sound of Daniel's quick, heavy breathing followed by an obligatory quick motion and increasingly loud moaning. Again and again she pressed her eyes shut and her fingers into her ears, but her naive hope that all this would turn out to be only a bad dream never came to pass. She was all alone with her horror. She had to be brave. Just one more time.

"Well, did you like it, Sandy? It won't be long now and you'll have hot adventures just like me."

Daniel pulled a handkerchief out of his jeans and, with an experienced motion, wiped his stomach.

"Maybe then you'll also be in the mood to tell me about it." Again that soft goat-like laughter.

"You are so mean. I've never done anything to hurt you. Tomorrow I'm going to tell mom."

Sandra's voice trembled from fear, shame, and indignation.

"You'll see what will happen then."

"Well, well, so you want to tell mom." His voice took on a threatening tone. "You are never going to do that.

Both of us know that you'll never tell anyone about this, ain't that so? You can't tell. If you do, you know what will happen? If you breathe just one single word, then I'll kill your shitty little guinea pig. I've warned you before. You love that little piece of shit. I'm warning you: one word, and your Daisy will be dead."

That was the cue for which Sandra had been waiting. So Daniel didn't know anything yet. She was trembling with excitement now that she could finally throw the liberating words at him. She had saved this moment until the very last. Her voice almost broke, as she told Daniel:

"This is the last time you are going to do this to me. You can't threaten me anymore. And you can't do anything to Daisy either …" She swallowed and said in a toneless voice:

"Daisy is dead."

For a moment the room fell silent. Sandra held her breath, then she saw Daniel jump up. "What do you mean, 'Daisy is dead'?" she heard Daniel hiss. "Are you trying to make me think that little shit is gone?" Disbelief and dismay were vibrating in his words.

"Yes. I did it. Now you'll never come here again and do those dirty things."

"What do you mean, you did it?"

"This afternoon I did it. In the garden. I was playing with Daisy and then …" Until now she had shown so much composure, hadn't even told her mother or grandmother anything, but now a coldness welled up inside her, making her slender body tremble. Her teeth were chattering, but she forced herself to explain. "I beat her on the head with a spade. As hard as I could. Several times." Then came the sentence which was the most important for Sandra, and she felt the cold and trembling subside. Very slowly and with exaggerated distinctness, triumphantly, she formulated her words.

"I did it … Now you can't do it anymore. You can't make me afraid again. And so, if you come into my room again, I can tell mom."

Daniel had not stirred during the last minute. Sandra could still make out his exact contours. She heard his breath come in quick, excited beats. After a seemingly endless moment he appeared to turn around and begin to leave.

Sandra knew that it was over, she had won. He would not come into her room anymore at night. The sacrifice had been cruel, but worth it.

"I will soon come back, my little sweetheart," he whispered to her. "And you won't tell mom anything. Because do you know what will happen, if you do?" The goat-like laughter wafted over to Sandra's bed.

"If you do talk," he repeated, "then … then you won't have a grandma for very long. You love the old bag, don't you? So remember: one word to mom and I'll kill grandma. Let me think, maybe I'll push her down the stairs. You can be dead sure that I'll do it, if you don't keep your trap shut! And now sleep well, my sweet little sister, and have pleasant dreams."

A soft chuckle and Daniel slipped out of her room like a shadow.

Under Ground, Out of Mind

Dirk is a heart specialist. No, no, not for broken hearts or anything like that, but a real specialist for heart ailments. He has his own practice. Outside there is a brass plate, inscribed Dr. Dirk Stein, M.D., cardiology, angiopathy, office hours by appointment. Dirk is a nice guy, and, besides, a good friend of mine, as are almost all men with whom I have had a relationship at one time or another. When I visit him in his office now and again, he always devotes a few minutes of his time to me. No matter how full the waiting room, he doesn't care.

We chat a bit; sometimes we neck as well and sometimes I bare my chest and he pretends to listen with his stethoscope, while actually stroking my breasts. I could laugh myself to death when I see how Linda turns pale when I stroll through the door. Linda is one of the girls who work for Dirk. She is head over heel in love with her boss. But that doesn't do her any good. I know that Dirk sleeps with her from time to time. But she doesn't mean a thing to him. Dirk only loves his mother. That's exactly the reason I left him.

He still lives with his mother at his parents' house. A man forty-one years old, just imagine! By the way, I've seen his mother a few times. She badmouthed me to him up one side and down the other. My skirts too short, my fingernails too long, my voice too deep for a woman, and God knows what else was wrong. Dirk always told me about it right away, and then we'd laugh. He's making piles of money, bought a Rolex for himself and his mother, drives a Ferrari, owns a fancy sailboat and a fantastic penthouse in Munich. That's where he often spends his weekends. Sometimes he takes me along with him.

Dirk throws his dough around a lot. Still, he's a nice guy, and we like each other from habit, if nothing else. Why am I telling all this about Dirk? Well, he is quite important to me. You see, I get the names and addresses from him.

Once there was a man among them who looked exactly like my third foster father. I was pretty startled when I saw him for the first time, since I didn't have good memories of Uncle Rudolf. He frequently beat me so bad that I really couldn't figure out how to sit down afterwards. Every evening I had to get beer for him at the little stand around the corner. Beer and cigarettes. Lucky Strikes without filters. He would smoke three packs a day, and the whole place stunk something awful.

So I went to bed early most of the time because when Uncle Rudolf had a few bottles in his belly, he was really unpredictable and it was better not to cross his path. Even when I held my ears, I often could hear how he and Aunt Ruth shouted at each other. Some days she had a black eye. I secretly enjoyed that because, you know, she often walloped me pretty good, too. Fortunately, at one point Aunt Ruth had had enough of me, and I could go back to the children's home.

Anyway, it's a little tricky with the names and addresses I get from Dirk. Of course if anyone ever knew that he gives them to me, he might have to close his practice on the spot and drive a cab. In the beginning it wasn't meant very seriously. We were in Munich one weekend, and we lazed around in the English Garden and played backgammon. He told me there that a patient of his had recently died. He had had three heart attacks already, and it caught up with him on his honeymoon. At a hotel in the Bahamas. His wife was almost thirty years younger and was suddenly, over night, a rich widow. That old fart told Dirk just a few months earlier that he had found a fantastic woman and felt totally young again because of her. Dirk said that he had warned him about his heart and so on. Sure he was happy for him because of his good luck, but he should be careful and not overdo it. Well, it didn't do a bit of good. At least the guy had a wonderful death. He literally, you know, kind of collapsed on top of his young wife. That wasn't much fun for his wife, but I think if you get so much money all of a sudden, you'd certainly get over it much faster. Dirk found out about all of this because he reads the obituaries. Suddenly the name of his patient popped up, and he called the widow and heard all about it.

At first I burst out laughing when I heard about it, but later I thought it over once more. This was a cool way to come into money.

Well, what else … I am now thirty-four years old and since last year a three-time widow. I own two houses, a one-family unit where I live, and a small apartment building in addition to a ranch in Spain. I have a super BMW, and I'm getting a fat pension since the death of my last husband. He was a medical director. Then there's all the rent money. So I sure can't complain.

Dirk is incredibly sweet; he doesn't ask for anything at all in return. I think he's simply happy to know that I am well-off. Maybe he's got a bad conscience because he won't ever untie himself from mom's apron strings, and he knows how much this has bothered me. I told him once already that I would wait for him till his mother's dead, but he turned completely pale and started to tremble. That was just a joke, I calmed him down and said let's hope that your mom lives to be at least a hundred, okay?

Dirk is really a very important person for me, at this point not because of the addresses but just because of the way he is. He understands me, pure and simple. Once I told him about my childhood and youth. Whoever brought me into this world didn't want me. At least I wasn't just dumped in the boonies, but in front of a church. I was wrapped in newspapers and was lying in a cardboard box. Luckily it was during the summer. At the hospital they named me Catherine. Come to think of it, quite pretty. As a kid I was constantly sick, had big problems with my skin and bronchial tubes. I scratched myself all the time and coughed till I was half dead. Probably not very attractive to adoptive parents. And the foster parents I lived with … it's better not to say anything about that, only that it amounted to nothing and I was better off at the children's home.

When I told this to Dirk, he actually started to cry. Somehow I found that very sweet of him. He always worries about me.

After school I started an apprenticeship as a legal secretary, but I didn't finish it. Then I decided to take on an apprenticeship as a baker and confectioner, baking fresh bread and decorating tortes and so on. All my life I have craved sweet stuff. I think that came about because sweetness was lacking in my life. But I've never had a problem with my figure. When I had really stuffed myself with sweets, I simply put a finger down my throat. I am very proud of the fact that I hardly ever do that anymore. Only rarely. Sometimes, I have to vomit for no reason, and I somehow always feel slightly nauseated. I saw a doctor about this and he told me it was entirely psychological. That's nonsense, of course. Don't I have a fantastic life? Anyway, I never went back to that doctor again.

I broke off that apprenticeship. Getting up so early was not for me, and it was better for my bronchial tubes as well, because of the flour dust and so on. Back then till my first marriage, I lived on welfare.

For some reason I don't really know what I want out of my life. I often lie in bed, my teddy bear in my arms, and make a mental picture of the people who might have been my parents. I imagine that both were absolutely beautiful. My mother had long blond hair and green eyes and looked like a movie star, perhaps like Brigitte Bardot, and my father was tall and slim, with dark hair, broad shoulders, and fantastic manners. The eyes I mention because I myself have light green eyes; I'm also tall – well, I must have gotten that from somewhere. Many men have told me that they consider me absolutely lovely, even beautiful, and I have to say, when I look in the mirror, I'm quite satisfied. Okay, my breasts could be a bit smaller and I'm not that happy with my thighs, but I really can't complain.

My parents – that topic is still painful to me. In the past I thought it would get better as I grew older, but I really fooled myself there. I can't help making up stories in my mind, again and again, about where I came from. I know when I'm doing it that it doesn't get me anywhere. I mean I have only my imagination to go on. No one is ever going to knock on my door and say: "How nice that I've finally found you! Your parents are the so-and-sos and they tried to find you all these years, because they've always missed you like crazy." Something like that only happens in fairy tales.

I believe it's really important to know where you come from; I mean where your roots are. It's much better to have some kind of family than none at all. And there's something else that's important too: even if I don't know where I come from, I should at least know where I'm going. There are times when I know exactly where I am going, and times that I also know precisely what I want.

But mostly I really don't. Then I live from day to day without a goal and wait for something exiting to happen. Most of the time nothing at all happens.

Often I stroll through the city and buy new threads and shoes; you see, I'm hung up on unusual shoes. Sometimes I buy presents for my friends and enjoy it when they're happy. Once in a while I invite them over and have a fantastic meal delivered. They like that and they feel at home. When they have all gone and I clean up, the thought strikes me that it would be nice if they would invite me over some time. But then, most of them have no money or too little space or something like that. If someone wants to hit me up for a loan, I find it hard to say no. My friends are all from earlier times, two from as far back as my days in the children's home. I want no contact with the relatives and friends of my dead husbands. Under ground, out of mind, I always say. But that sounds worse than I really mean. My three husbands weren't so bad, after all, especially the last one. I think I really loved this one. Of course I had the phone numbers of many men. Some of them I met. But I wouldn't have married just anyone, only because they had a lot of dough; I had to like him as well. And mainly I had to be able to imagine going to bed with him. You see, I couldn't do that with someone I considered unattractive.

Their age was a problem, of course; they were all retired cardiac cases. When they heard that I had grown up in a children's home and never had a happy family life – this immediately triggered their protective instincts.

Truly moving! So I became their little girl whose every wish they anticipated. During the day I was the little girl they watched over, and at night I wore them out, I mean the first two of them. I was insatiable. Of course they were afraid to take Viagra because of their hearts, but I didn't give a damn. Hey – they shouldn't have married a young woman. What happened to the woman in the Bahamas luckily never happened to me.

Ed was my first husband, a lawyer at one time, a widower, a bit eggheaded, but otherwise nice enough. We had been married for only half a year when he slumped down while watching the news and was dead. I called Dirk and he came over right away and filled out the death certificate. My second husband owned a factory; he was set on having a baby with me. Well, I said, in that case he should really put out, and, secretly of course, I took the pill. He was divorced and had a grown son. All his hopes had been on this son. But he died in a motorcycle accident. That happened two years before we got to know each other. Lothar was crazy jealous. He almost never let me out of his sight. He wanted us to do everything together. So I took him to a disco. He didn't notice how ridiculous he made himself appear. On the evening that he had a stroke in the middle of the dance floor, I had just gone to the toilet. When I dance so wildly and sweat, I like to have ice-cold water run across my forearms. That is absolutely refreshing. When I came back to the dance-floor I had just become a widow for the second time. We had been married for a little longer than a year.

Then I took a break. I had to digest this, and financially I was doing quite well. But at some point, I think after about two years, I felt the urge again and asked Dirk whether he didn't know someone for me. He gave me the names of three guys and told me a little about them, and I knew right away that only one of them interested me. This was the retired medical director that I've mentioned. Dirk described him in such a nice way, his sense of humor and his good manners; besides he was supposed to be a very attractive man. When I got to know Josef, I knew immediately that I wanted to marry him as soon as possible. It took only a few months till he asked, like a gentleman, for my hand in marriage. Josef was a wonderful man, and he was the only one that I felt really sad about his sick heart. So we didn't sleep together very often, and when we did, it was very gently and carefully. Our evenings were nicest of all. When we went to sleep, he kissed me on both my eyes. Then I turned over on my side and held my teddy bear in my arms, and Josef was lying behind me and took both me and the teddy bear into his arms. Then he told me stories. He had a fantastic voice. It was so wonderful to fall asleep in his arms. I felt completely safe and secure. After we had been married for four years, I lost him. Late one evening, in a parking garage, a junkie beat him to a pulp and robbed him. A few hours later he died in a hospital. That's now a year ago and I just can't forget him. I especially miss him in the evenings when I lie in bed with cold feet. Josef always had really warm hands and feet. Just like a human oven. Oh Josef …

Actually I am now pretty well off. When I lived on welfare, I was always afraid I would end up in the gutter and, even worse, that there would be nobody who would care at all. But today this isn't true. First, I now have enough money, and second, I know that Dirk at least would be totally unhappy if I were bad off. He doesn't want to have anything to do with my other friends. Well, that's his loss; I won't butt in. Also he never comes to my parties. I think he loves me and doesn't even know it.

I have made up my mind that I am finished with men. I don't want to marry again. Doing that takes a lot out of me and wears me out. Besides – now I have everything I wanted. I can't be anything but happy. Right?

Deceit

Berlin, June 14th

Dear Claudia,

Well, how are you? Did you have a nice birthday party? Believe me, I really would have liked to join your party and stay for a long weekend, but it was, of all things, the weekend for which George had planned an "advanced training course" in Hamburg, and you know how little time we have for each other.

Oh Claudia, I don't feel at all well right now. I've been together with George for three years now. That surely is cause for celebration, but on the other hand ... I would never have thought it possible, but I have become so attached to this man that I can't imagine life without him anymore. Lately I catch myself thinking more and more often how wonderful it would be to wake up every morning at his side. When he returns home in the evening, I feel I could burst into tears at any moment.

I'm asking myself why he is still with that woman. He always says it's because of Jonas. But after all, Jonas is now 16. At that age he scarcely needs George anymore. It's a time when girls, pals and sports fill a boy's head. But that's the way George is, very conscious of his responsibilities. In a couple of years, he always says, things will look quite different. But so will I. I'm not all that young anymore, and I sure won't become more attractive. Oh Claudia, I don't feel like spending my life in a holding pattern.

June 15th

Claudia, I need your advice. Matters can't go on like this forever. Something entered my mind, but I am not quite sure yet whether I should go through with it. I've been thinking what could induce George to get a divorce. And I think I have found a solution. You know of course that George has been given a six-week work assignment in the US. Last week we held a farewell get-together. I could kill my boss for not giving me some time off during those six weeks. But her practice is totally chaotic. Imagine, she even collapsed right in the treatment room recently. But that's another story. So if I were to write George now that I am pregnant, then he would have the time and distance to reflect on everything. And when he returns home, he can tell his wife how matters stand. In the meanwhile he can figure out how he can best extricate himself from that marriage. Of course I don't have a hundred-percent assurance that he will decide in my favor, but I have a good feeling about that. Besides, this is better than waiting years for better times. George is so considerate and loving that he surely would not abandon me. And if he does, despite everything – I'm prepared to put all my eggs in one basket.

If it works, I can always pretend later that I had a miscarriage. And who knows, perhaps George and I really will have a child together. At any rate I don't have a lot of time left.

The most important thing for me now is to get George to put his cards on the table. I started this letter saying I need your advice. But if I really think about it, I only need your emotional support. What do you think about this whole matter? I'm almost sure now that this is how I'll handle it, just as I wrote it. At times it helps to put something on paper and then a decision comes more easily. It just has to work! Oh Claudia, keep your fingers crossed for me. If my letter sounds a bit chaotic, excuse me, but I'm pretty agitated. Please respond quickly!

Love and many regards from your Irene

Frankfurt, June 17th

You crazy fool, what outlandish things are you planning? You are asking for my honest opinion? Okay, here it is: I think this idea is absolutely stupid. May I remind you that you knew precisely what you were letting yourself in for when you plunged into this affair with George! I told you at the time that problems might arise, but you kept insisting that your independence meant so much to you. To have an affair with a married man is fantastic, you said. You are *being pampered, you have no obligations, and you don't have to bother with his dirty laundry. Well, love seems to have double-crossed you now. During the last few months I saw something like this coming. You did almost nothing on weekends but sit around at home waiting for his furtive calls. What happened to your much-beloved freedom? Has it become unimportant to you all of a sudden?*

Without a question, I find what you intend to do quite risky. I met George only once and that was two years ago, but I don't believe he would forgive you for a trick like this, if he should ever catch on. Okay, I could be mistaken; after all I really only know him from your descriptions and letters, but I don't have a good feeling about this whole affair. Besides, he knows very well that you've been taking the pill for many years because of your hormonal imbalance. And then getting pregnant all of a sudden? How are you going to explain that?

My dear Irene, think it over one more time. I can understand your impatience about having everything out in the open. But does it have to be like this? Besides, it would be quite different if he chose you without your being pregnant, don't you think? Of course, he is cheating on his wife, but in my opinion he still does not deserve to be misled like this. After all, he has always been straight with you. Mull it over once more, very carefully, and ask yourself whether there isn't another way.

Fondly, Claudia

Berlin, June 20th

My beloved George,

You can't imagine how much I miss you. It's still a whole long month until we see each other again. How am I going to bear that?! One month without your glances, your kisses, your hands …

Do you miss me a little? With all the meetings and business meals do you have any chance at all to think of me?

My darling, what I have to tell you can't be postponed until I see you again. I simply cannot bear to wait until then. George, I have no idea how to begin; it's so unbelievable. This morning I went to see Dr. Meinrad, my gynecologist. And he told me that I'm pregnant. George, I am going to have a baby! I can't explain it, because I've been taking the pill for years. Dr. Meinrad asked me whether I have been sick recently, so I told him that some weeks ago I had a horrible stomach infection with vomiting and diarrhea. That was during a week when we didn't see each other and this is the reason I didn't tell you about it. I didn't want to worry you. Anyway, Dr. Meinrad said that in such circumstances the pill can fail, because it does not stay in the body long enough to be effective. Well, medical explanations don't help now. I myself can't believe it yet, but it happened. I am pregnant!

Oh darling, we felt so secure and we never talked about this subject, since you knew I had to take the pill. I am so confused. I only learned this a few hours ago. What are we going to do now?

One thing I know for sure: I did not wish for this child, but it would break my heart to have an abortion. After all it is your child as well. And how could I refuse to have the child of a man I love so much! George, my darling, how I would love to lie in your arms now and hear you say that everything will turn out all right! I long for you so much. I'm sorry that I'm telling you like this. Believe me, I would much rather have told you this in person while holding you tight, but I really can't bear to hold this back for a whole month. Can you understand this? I'm so looking forward to the moment when we see each other again. I need you. We need you.

I love you more than anything in the world.
All yours, Irene

Los Angeles, June 29th

Irene,

I received your letter the day before yesterday. I read it with great consternation. To be sure, for reasons other than the ones you surmise. Irene, I could never have imagined that you would be capable of something like this. We have been together now for three years. We have loved and trusted one another – and then you betray me in such a shabby way?! My disappointment knows no bounds. You have succeeded in destroying my feelings for you. How could you have done this?!

But I don't want to keep you in suspense any longer. If your gynecologist tells you that you are pregnant, it's prob-

ably the case. But one thing I can tell you: that child is certainly not my child. It cannot, in any circumstances, be mine. I want you to know why. When I was in my early twenties I contracted mumps. Normally it's a childhood disease and not dangerous in any way. If one contracts it in later years, however, it can lead to infertility. And exactly that happened in my case. I found out about ten years ago. Andrea and I had wished for a child for a long time. When it didn't happen, I had myself examined. I am infertile. As far as Jonas is concerned, you can figure out by yourself that he is not my biological son. When I met Andrea, she was pregnant with him. It never bothered me. I was present when he was born and I brought him up. To me, Jonas is my son.

Irene, I don't know if you dreamed up that entire story or if you actually expect a child by another man; but either way it no longer interests me. It would be pointless for us to meet again. I couldn't trust you anymore.

Farewell, George

Berlin, July 8ᵗʰ

Dear Sonya,

I don't want to beat endlessly around the bush, but will come straight to the point, especially since I couldn't get you on the phone. I'm in a terrible situation and don't know which way to turn. Sonya, I am pregnant. Good God, what shall I do? I've been with Jeff for two years now. Everything has been running so smoothly; his wife is often traveling on business, and she suspects no more than my husband. *Jeff and I never planned for a future together. Why should we have? Now and again a nice evening together – that was enough for us. What on earth will happen now?*

I can't imagine having an abortion, but once I have the baby, I can immediately file for divorce. It's far easier for other women in my situation. In Germany it's said that one child in ten is an extramarital child. But I certainly cannot foist a child on him, because he had mumps in his early twenties and is infertile. Oh, why of all things did something like this happen to me?! In a few days George will be returning from the US. I'll have to come to a decision by then. Please get in touch with me as soon as possible or I'll crack up …

Andrea

Class Reunion

Barbara Anderson was a merry widow. She would never have labeled herself that way and would have considered any remark to that effect as being in bad taste and indignantly rejected it. In fact she had slowly, but noticeably, blossomed after her husband's death. Once a week she visited him at the cemetery, brought a small bouquet of fresh flowers along, and discarded the withered ones. Occasionally she caught herself whistling a little song during her task and immediately fell silent.

Her happiness must have been out of place somehow. Her marriage certainly had not been the very best, but it hadn't been really bad either. By and large she and her husband had gone their separate ways. Not that they had been unfaithful to one another. At least in that respect Mrs. Anderson could vouch for herself.

She would not have been able to say as much for her husband, certainly not for the first years of their marriage, but that did not interest her any more. In her imagination he was buzzing about somewhere above, observing her. From time to time she abruptly looked up toward heaven and stuck out her tongue.

Donald Anderson had been a postal clerk. All day long he sat behind a glass pane, weighed letters, sold stamps, received packages, and drew very neat lines with the help of a ruler. All that had not benefited his figure. Over the years his backside had eclipsed his wife's and his chest began right above the belt.

To add to his misfortunes he met a fate that he shared with many men. His dark-brown, once full head of hair had begun to fall out in his early thirties. At first he grew an enormous moustache, but after a colleague had quipped that people could see what he had for lunch, he immediately shaved it off. Instead he let the remaining hair grow and each morning combed the strands from one side of his pate to the other. He battened down the whole assembly with his wife's fixative. Once, when he audibly pondered the acquisition of a toupee, she threatened to divorce him.

Donald was not clumsy. He was able to repair cars and toasters and he sang in a church choir. Now and again he took a walk in a forest to gather mushrooms. While doing this he once discovered a corpse, an event he would talk about for a long time and which was probably the most exciting of his life. Every Friday evening he met with a colleague, a neighbor and a basso from his choir, at his bar for a game of cards. He would sometimes return from these occasions not entirely sober. Barbara generously ignored it. One couldn't have everything; at least he did not smoke. How often she heard her neighbor complain about her yellowed curtains which constantly had to be washed, a problem she did not have.

Once a year Donald and Barbara and their two daughters went on vacation together to the coast of the North Sea. When the girls reached the age when they preferred to spend their vacations at a girl-scout camp in France, their parents at first gave their permission only reluctantly. But after the two returned tanned and rested, the couple was reassured and afterwards spent their vacations by themselves.

Barbara succeeded in convincing her husband to consider a different vacation site only once. She had discovered an exceptionally inexpensive offer in Tunisia: a four-star hotel with a swimming pool right on the beach. Donald considered his wife to be reckless and only after many attempts at persuasion did he finally give in. The vacation turned into a fiasco. Donald got the worst sunburn of his life, then an upset stomach. To top it off, his camera was snatched. He swore that if he survived this one, he would never again go on vacation anywhere other than the good old North Sea. He survived. Barbara asked herself whether this was all that would ever happen. To her chagrin, it was.

Barbara had a part-time job as a clerk in an office. When their daughters were becoming more independent, she began thinking about herself again. Once a week she met with some women friends for a cup of coffee. She crisscrossed her neighborhood on a bicycle and devotedly gave herself over to gardening on her small property at the outskirts of town. Beyond this she went swimming once in a while or read a novel. But she liked nothing better than to spend time in the little garden which Donald and she had leased for more than twenty years. This piece of property required a lot of work. Donald's collaboration confined itself to mowing the lawn and painting the bower. But when Barbara had harvested zucchinis thicker than those of all her neighbors, she came home aglow with happiness and contentment. Then nothing and nobody could upset her. Not even Donald.

His death came suddenly. Donald was sitting on his orthopedic chair in the post office and had just stamped a letter, when his body tipped forward and his forehead hit the desk. Stroke. When Barbara later caught sight of him with the stamp mark on his forehead, she cried out, and then burst out in hysterical laughter, which finally gave way to uncontrollable sobbing. She pressed a kiss upon his forehead, just above the stamp mark, noisily blew her nose once more, and went away. She took a deep breath and resolved not to cry anymore. And that was that. Now their two daughters had to be notified and the funeral arranged. Barbara had often heard about chiselers in the funeral business. They assumed that in such circumstances people would not think clearly and could be talked into all sorts of things. Not her. Back at home she looked for funeral parlors in her neighborhood and asked only one question: How much do you charge for the cheapest coffin? You see, the deceased is to be cremated, so a cheap coffin will do. Most of the parlors gave out that information with great reluctance, but despite that, Barbara managed to learn what she needed to know. The difference in price was enormous. For a simple pine-wood coffin, the most expensive undertaker wanted € 700, the cheapest only € 200. Barbara settled upon a date. She poured herself a glass of sherry, sipped and closed her eyes. So that was that. This is how it feels to be a widow.

On the day Donald Anderson met his maker, Richard and Edith Miller celebrated their silver anniversary. There really wasn't much to celebrate, but they did not want to disappoint their family, friends, and neighbors and had rented the clubhouse of the garden-plot society. The women had baked cakes and pies, and for dinner a cold and warm buffet was brought in from a catering service.

Close to sixty guests had come. It came off like most of the parties in the club house: the air was sticky from smoke and other noxious odors, beer flowed like water, cream pies and roast pork were consumed greedily. Fat Karl accompanied it all on his electronic organ with hit tunes from the seventies.

Children ran around between the tables; the men had already loosened their ties and the women were surreptitiously inspecting the jewelry and wardrobes of their female companions. The later the hour, the more ribald the jokes. During lulls the men turned to serious subjects such as politics and soccer. A few couples turned circles on the dance floor, but only now and then, because

Karl's repertoire wasn't exactly extensive: Some songs he was now playing for the fifth time. That is to say, when he was playing at all – because the music was coming more and more often from the CD-player. Meanwhile Fat Karl was sitting next to his fat Norma and his head was turning redder and redder from the beer and the heat.

When the celebration was drawing to a close, Richard gave a short speech and thanked everybody for the beautiful presents.

Cleaning up was to take place next morning. Little by little Richard and Edith said goodbye to their guests. Several gift baskets were piled up on a table in a corner of the room. The items, from basket to basket, scarcely differed from one another: liquor, ham, chocolate. They had fulfilled their purpose by eliciting disingenuous, admiring "Ohs" from the celebrating couple. Tomorrow the items would be picked up by car.

It was two a.m. when Richard and Edith, exhausted, fell on their bed. While Edith was snoring loudly a few minutes later, Richard lay awake for a long time, reflecting. They had been married now for twenty-five years. "And for how long must you keep going on?" some wit had asked him that evening. Indeed, this question had secretly occurred to Richard as well. Their childless marriage bobbed up and down steadily for years: once a year a three-week vacation in Bavaria, once a month a halfhearted intercourse, once a week a visit from his mother-in-law, and at least once a day a vociferous argument.

That was supposed to be it? It was.

Nearly a year after the funeral and the silver anniversary, Barbara Anderson and Richard Miller received identical pieces of mail. Margot Lange took pleasure in announcing that once again ten years had passed and the next class reunion was imminent. While Barbara had attended all reunions, Richard so far had felt no desire to see his former classmates again.

Nonetheless he had politely responded to every invitation and had twice given Margot Lange his new address. Perhaps he would attend the event at some point after all.

This year's reunion was scheduled for June 29th; replies were requested by June 1st. It fitted in neatly with Barbara's plans. She wanted to fly to Mallorca for two weeks with a widow she had met when swimming. They would return on June 26th. During the last week in May she picked up her phone and called Margot in order to accept. Much to her consternation she learned that Paul Mertens would not be with them. His wife had informed Margot that the antique dealer had died of lung cancer last May. Barbara sighed and thought wistfully of the charming man who always had a cigarette in the corner of his mouth and an impish saying on his lips. What a pity; she had flirted with him so memorably every ten years. Paul had wanted to see Barbara again after the class reunions, but she consistently turned him down. After all, both of them were married. Unfortunately not to one another, as she sometimes thought regretfully.

Well, now the time had come around once again. How fast, indeed, the ten years had passed. As one got older, time simply flew by.

Tanned and excited, Barbara took the suburban train to the downtown area, where the class reunion was to take place in a restaurant. Her heart beat faster as she nervously stroked her full blond hair outside the entrance.

"Hello, beautiful lady. Are you also on your way to the class reunion?" Suddenly hearing this voice and surprised, she turned around. Surely that was … Now what was his name? Very good in math, however entirely unmusical. Barbara, embarrassed, smiled at the slender man with his graying temples.

"I'm sorry, I have forgotten your name," she admitted candidly, while extending her hand to him. "I only remember that you sat one row ahead of me and sometimes secretly read a book hidden underneath the bench."

"Bull's eye. My name is Miller, Richard Miller, and you are Barbara Berg, the girl with the thick pigtail." They were still standing in front of the restaurant and made no move to go inside.

"Right," Barbara smiled, "except that my name is Anderson now."

"Well, shall we go inside and see who else from the old gang is there?" Richard held the door for her and gestured invitingly.

He looks good, the thought flashed through Barbara's mind, causing her to blush. As soon as she walked in, she heard the noisy group which had been placed in a back room of the restaurant. People had ample space there, and they could have some privacy. She walked toward her classmates at Richard Miller's side. Both were greeted with a boisterous "Hello." Richard in particular caught the attention of the others, because scarcely anyone had seen him since their time together in school.

The class reunion took its usual course. After the group was completely assembled, everyone gave his name and reported briefly about his or her family and career. Following that, people recalled old times, told anecdotes, laughed, lauded, and tattled. Six former classmates were dead, three were not able to come, and the retired teacher, Hermann Crick, called 'cricket' by all, had died at the blessed age of eighty-nine. He had been present at the last class reunion and had performed, to the amusement of everyone, some poems by the humorist Ringelnatz.

It gave Barbara a bit of a jolt that Richard was married. Inwardly, she scolded herself for that. Since Donald's death she had taken no interest in other men. She had met a widower at the cemetery whom she immediately liked. After greeting each other for weeks they had exchanged a few words. But soon the man began to annoy Barbara, because he talked about nothing but his late wife and complained bitterly that now he had to look after himself. Apparently his wife had taken care of virtually everything and he resented the fact that he was now thrown onto his own resources.

By contrast Richard Miller made a very different impression; he was worldly and self-assured, well-groomed and sensitive, with beautiful hands and teeth that looked as if they were still his own.

That's strange, Barbara thought, when they were classmates Richard had never caught her attention. He was one of the shy and reserved pupils who put off strangers, even if, over the years, their faces became familiar.

In the course of the evening, small groups began to form, some of them cliques that existed during their school years. Richard hovered over Barbara the entire evening, wanting to know everything about her life, her daughters, her work, her health, and how she was managing since Donald's death.

Barbara enjoyed his attentiveness, and when she was about to order a cab shortly after midnight, Richard stopped her and offered to drive her home. He had drunk very little that evening because he had come with his car, so Barbara finally consented. They said goodbye to everyone and, given the advanced age of the group, an agreement was reached to have the next meeting take place in only five years. From the corners of her eyes she saw how people were whispering when they, accompanied by good wishes, were leaving the reunion together.

Barbara told him her address and was happy that they would be able to continue their conversation for a few minutes more.

"Over there," Barbara said, "the second house to the right." Richard parked his car directly in front of the small townhouse and turned off the motor. Barbara felt her heart beating. He leaned toward her and by the bright light of the street lamp she could see he was smiling.

"May I come in with you for awhile?" Richard asked and reached for her hand.

"I … I don't know," Barbara stammered, "whether this is such a good idea."

"Of course it's a good idea," Richard calmed her and breathed a kiss on the back of her hand. "Just for a few minutes. We'll drink a small glass of wine as a farewell and then I'll be on my way."

"Very well, then," Barbara gave in. To be sure, Richard had not convinced her, but why create difficulties now, she thought, trying to assuage her concerns. It had been a very nice evening, and, after all, she had known this man since childhood.

Richard smiled and winked at her before stepping out of the car and, completely the gentleman, opening the car door for her. He nonchalantly placed his arm around her waist during the few steps to her house.

Simultaneous, fear and delight made her shiver. The neighbor's place was dark. She hoped that Mrs. Kamps, the preeminent gossip of the entire street, was asleep. This woman sometimes knew things about people before such thoughts had even entered one's own mind.

It was only on the third try that Barbara found the keyhole. While still in the hallway, Richard pulled her close and tried to kiss her. She resisted, but only a little. What would he think of her, if she allowed him to kiss her without offering any resistance? His kisses became more insistent, his hands more daring. How long had it been since she had experienced such passion! Decades. During a short breathing spell she let Richard know that she didn't want to remain in the hallway any longer and so, kissing and breathing heavily, they approached the broad couch in the living room. Richard was half lying on top of her and beginning to unbutton her blouse. At the same time Barbara felt one of his hands gliding beneath her skirt. This man was like an octopus. So many hands seemed to touch her that she had no idea where to begin repulsing them.

"Richard …" she murmured softly at first, then more loudly. "Richard!" The man paused. Barbara groped for the switch on the lamp in the corner of the living room. Her breathing was heavy, the knot of his tie had gone askew.

"What is the matter, darling?" Richard asked. Just hearing his warm voice made Barbara melt.

"Richard," Barbara started anew, while carefully detaching herself from his embrace. "This is all going a bit too fast for me." She hesitated. "Perhaps you would like something to drink." The last word had scarcely been uttered when Richard closed her mouth with a kiss. At the same time he lifted Barbara up. She would not have imagined him being so strong. "Come on, my sweetheart," Richard whispered in her ear. "We will go to your bedroom, okay?" Barbara did not answer and looked at him with wide-open eyes. "We will lie down on your bed and I will simply hold you in my arms. I'll do nothing that you don't want as well."

When there was no protest, Richard carried her to the stairway. At the very first step he stumbled and could keep his balance only with some effort.

"You had better put me down," she giggled. "You've got to get used to these steps. They turn out to be a bit too steep."

Richard carefully put her down; they climbed up the steps one behind the other, and pulling him after her, Barbara entered the bedroom. It was a funny feeling. Never had she been in this room with another man. Thank God that she had made the bed this morning! Richard looked around briefly, took off his jacket and his shoes, and loosened his tie. He let himself drop down on the bed and patted the mattress. "Come on now, Barbara." For a moment she struggled with herself. She looked at this attractive man, thought about Donald, the neighbors, and her reputation. Then curiosity triumphed. She kicked off her pumps and lay down next to him. Richard pulled her toward him. After a while he kissed her again. When he continued tampering with her buttons, she did likewise. The hairs on his chest were grey and for a man his age he had an astonishingly flat stomach. Barbara could smell traces of his shaving lotion. Oh, how beautiful all this was! What a pleasure it was to be desired. No, she was not going to think of consequences. She had already decided on that. Who knows? Tomorrow a roof tile might fall on her head or a bus might run her over. She was living now! And she was passionately determined to enjoy these hours.

"Sparkling wine," she whispered. "I have a bottle of sparkling wine in the fridge. Should we break it open?" Expectantly she looked at Richard.

"Good idea," he murmured and placed a kiss on the tip of her nose. "You probably put it in there, because you thought, well, let's see who I drag home from the class reunion. Am I right?"

Barbara laughed along with him. "That's exactly how it was. Are you a mind reader?" She released herself from his arms and prepared to get up.

"No, no. You just stay here," Richard was already sitting on the edge of the bed. "I'll get the bottle. All you have to do is let me know where I'll find the kitchen and two glasses."

"The kitchen is directly opposite the stairs, you can't miss it. The glasses are in the wall cupboard next to the door."

"I'll be right back. Don't run away. Do I get a goodbye kiss?"

Barbara stretched toward him and smiled. What a captivating man he was! No thought now of his wife. That would only spoil her mood. She looked after him, as he was leaving the bedroom in his stockinged feet.

"The light switch for the staircase is to the left of the bedroom door," she called out. She saw the light go on and leaned back, relaxed. Would he like her looks? She thought back on the admiring glances which he had secretly cast at her all evening long and she smiled, satisfied. What good luck that she had sparkling wine in

the fridge. It was rare that she had wine; the bottle had really been intended for a girlfriend who had watered her flowers during her vacation. She had just not gotten around to giving it to her.

While Barbara listened to Richard moving around in the kitchen, she decided to create a romantic mood. Because they knew their mother liked listening to music before going to sleep, her daughters had given her a CD-player as a gift for her bedroom. She liked classical music best, sometimes operettas as well, but that would not be appropriate now. Barbara quickly looked through her CD's and fixed on 'Tenderly' by Cleo Laine. That was just the right thing, seductive and soft and wonderful to dream by. The first piano tones were playing, when she heard Richard coming up the stairs. Barbara smiled expectantly. The dimmed light made her gold-brown skin glisten and appear soft as velvet.

It was an ugly noise that startled her. Breaking glass, a brief outcry, rumbling sounds, then the most terrible, utter silence. She listened, holding her breath.

"Richard," she cried out, stricken with fear, "Richard!"

In a single leap she was out of bed and running to the narrow hallway. She saw him immediately. He was lying at the foot of the stairs in a curiously twisted position. The staircase was strewn with shattered glass; the sweet smell of sparkling wine lingered in the air. Barbara ran back to the bedroom, put on her pumps, and rushed down the stairs. Richard was lying half on the stairs and half on the floor. With a great effort Barbara turned him on his back, whispering his name again and again. His head no longer seemed to belong to him, attached to his torso only by his skin, not the spine.

She looked into his blood-covered face and turned cold. A piece of glass protruded from his forehead, exactly in the place where the stamp imprint had been on Donald's forehead.

The House Across the Street

The thermometer inside the room stood at 32 degrees Centigrade. The insulation was truly terrible. A typical attic apartment: in winter an icebox, in summer a furnace. And this summer was brutally hot. Even the nights didn't bring any relief; not a breeze blowing anywhere.

I don't believe much in fans. I catch cold easily, so it doesn't make much sense to install such a rotating monster. That's why my windows are open only during the night and during the early morning hours in the hot months. When it is as hot as it can be on these days, I can keep the room dark if need be. And to insure privacy, I don't need the plastic blinds because my apartment and the one next door, where my girlfriend lives, are situated higher than all the other apartments in the neighborhood. Also, I'm not interested in what's happening in the lives of other people. I don't have even a nodding acquaintance with the people living on the other side of the street.

Even in my dreams I would never imagine the enchanting drama that I experienced during a quick glance, of all things, at the house across the street, a performance which every man would envy me for. Again and again I remember it with a smile.

On the day in question the heat was nearly unbearable. I had stripped down to my underwear. The wet towels that I had placed on all the radiators had long dried out and I was collecting them in order to hold them under the faucet again. As I was getting the towel from the bedroom I heard a bang from the street.

I reached out reflexively, pushed the window up a bit and looked down. Nothing extraordinary. Just a backfire.

Then my glance fell on the top floor of the house across the street. A few days before a moving van had been parked there. There were no curtains and I could see everything. I had no idea who might be living there. I saw a double bed, a large clothes closet and a rectangular mirror, about the height of a man, which stood on the floor next to the clothes closet. Between the door and the bed there was a lot of space.

I was just about to shut the window when I saw her enter the room. She was at most twenty years old and nearly nude. Her body was perfect, as far as I could judge from my vantage point. Long slender legs, a well-formed behind, which a tiny dark pair of panties emphasized more than concealed, a narrow waistline, medium-sized firm breasts, curly brown hair, which fell softly and abundantly upon her shoulders. A pretty face. She held something in her right hand as she entered the room, and I recognized it as a plastic bottle with body lotion. She placed the bottle on the bed and swayed back and forth like a dancer. Looking at her simply took your breath away. A wondrously beautiful girl who danced, nearly without clothes, in front of a mirror. I couldn't hear the music but I saw what it produced. How supple were her motions, how pliant her immaculate body. I took only shallow breaths and remained motionless, as though I feared she would see me if I made the slightest movement. That wasn't in fact possible, because I observed her through the narrow space between the wooden frame and the shade.

The dancer reached for the bottle, unscrewed the cap, and pressed the white milky fluid into her hand. Then, still dancing, she started to apply the lotion to her suntanned body. First to her hands, then the forearms, the elbows, finally the upper arms. Her fingers glided over her neck and journeyed to her breasts, upon which she gently spread the fluid while observing herself in the mirror and turning her head coquettishly back and forth. Pure joy of living and youthful vigor, an incarnate ray of sunshine that lit up the entire room. Her hands moved in circular motions across her flat belly, stroked her hips, and tried reaching her back. Between applications, with the bottle in her hands, rotating motions, dance steps, swaying, quivering.

I felt shabby, but I was unable to resist. Quick as lightning I got a pair of binoculars from the next room and fervently hoped that I would enjoy this gorgeous view for yet a while longer. While I focused the binoculars, the young Aphrodite set one foot on the edge of the bed and spread the lotion on her legs. After she had massaged everything, she devoted herself to her feet. When she had completed her task, she began again to dance in front of the mirror, lightly, as though gliding on air.

Unfortunately the show came to an end when I saw Mark parking in front of the house. He had mentioned his intention to come today in order to connect a more up-to-date, faster modem. Regretfully, I lowered the binoculars and reached for the thin cotton dress that I had already laid out on my bed.

I could have shown him, of course, what had so brightened the last twenty minutes for me, but it wouldn't have been worth the effort. My grandson is gay.

Promises

"Okay, okay, I'm coming, I'm coming. An old woman is no race horse!"

Slowly Elsa moved toward the telephone, then carried it into the spacious kitchen where she had been preoccupied with solving a crossword puzzle. Only after comfortably settling herself at the table did she finally pick up the receiver.

"Elsa Schwarz."

"It's me. I'm just coming from the hospital," Elsa heard her sister exclaim with a long sigh of relief.

"Martin is out of the woods. He's out of intensive care. My prayers must have helped."

A contented smile crossed Elsa's face. "Thank God. For once we're getting good news. How's he doing? Is he in a lot of pain?"

"They've filled him up with pain killers. Most of the time I just sit next to his bed and stroke his hand. He's so pale, and his face is so thin," Gertrud sobbed. "It's just terrible to see your own child in such a state."

"He pulled through, you said. That's all that counts. You shouldn't excite yourself so much, Gertrud. You have to think of your health. You know the doctor told you to avoid any kind of excitement. It was hard enough to break the news of Martin's accident to you. I was scared you'd have a heart attack."

Noisily Gertrud blew her nose. "Sure, sure, everything's all right now. The rascal got away with it." Elsa reached for her large coffee cup with its floral design and took a swallow with obvious pleasure.

"Say, how long are you going to stay in Munich anyway?"

"I have no idea. I'll stay as long as Martin needs me here. I'll have to see, one or two weeks, perhaps even longer. You can manage without me, can't you?"

Elsa nodded. "Listen, don't worry about me. You may be younger than I am, but it's *you* who has the weak heart. I've got to take care of *you,* not the other way around. Of course I can manage things here by myself. It's just that it'll be strange here without you." She took another sip from her coffee. "Tell me a bit more about Martin. Does he have a nice roommate?"

"Yes, a Latin teacher. Early fifties, I would guess, about Martin's age. He makes a nice impression, and he promised me that he would keep an eye on Martin. By the way, I talked to the doctor a while ago. She said the head injury is less severe than his leg troubles. It was a really complicated operation. In about a year he's got to go back to the hospital so they can take out those horrible screws and bolts. Good grief, why did that boy have to have such bad luck!" Gertrud sounded depressed.

"Well. That can't be changed now. The main thing is that he recovers fully. As I always say ..." Elsa hesitated for a moment, "if you play with fire, you get burned. I'm sorry, but it was out and out crazy to go roller-skating at his age." Elsa, despite all her sympathy for her nephew, could not hold her opinion in check.

Gertrud was annoyed. "It's called in-line skating. And why do you have to start in about that all over again? If that's his idea of a good time, then let him do it! He gets his exercise and is outdoors. Why begrudge him his fun!"

"Of course, of course," Elsa replied in a conciliatory tone. "Will you call me again tomorrow? Same time as today?"

"Sure, and what are you going to do this evening?"

Elsa let her glance sweep the room indecisively. "Don't know yet. Maybe I'll watch a movie and finish knitting that sweater. Or play the piano. I'll see. Till tomorrow evening then, Gertrud. And give Martin my best."

Without waiting for an answer she put down the receiver. The last swallow of coffee had already turned cool. Elsa got up awkwardly and poured the rest into the soil of her flowerpot. That was good for the plants. She put the empty cup into the sink, which was already stacked with dirty dishes from the last three days. Elsa had not been in the mood to wash dishes. She enjoyed letting things go. It wouldn't be long now before Gertrud returned, and with her, order and cleanliness.

She replaced the telephone on the small chest of drawers in the hallway and put on a cardigan. Then she returned to the kitchen and started preparing her supper. Taking a plate in one hand and a glass of grape juice in the other, she walked to the living room, turned on the television, leaned back and relaxed. The news had just begun. Elsa, only mildly interested, watched the ceremonies celebrating the first anniversary of Germany's reunification in 1989. Chewing on the last radish, she picked up the TV schedule. Today, as so often, there was nothing she really wanted to watch. "Stupid box," Elsa muttered, frustrated, and turned it off. She returned the plate and glass to the kitchen. It was still early evening. She could sit down in the comfortable wing chair and continue reading the novel she had started, but she wasn't really in the mood. Instead, how about playing the piano for a bit? She hadn't done that in weeks. The piano stool creaked as she sat down and slowly and deliberately lifted the lid from the keys. Soft waltz-like tunes filled the house, as Elsa hummed along. She knew only a few pieces by heart, and her repertoire was quickly exhausted. Ill-humored, she leafed through the few music books lying on the piano. They were not what she had in mind. How many years had it been since she had played a sonatina? However, the music books were not downstairs, but somewhere in the attic. Should she call her sister to ask where she'd find them? After all, the attic was Gertrud's territory. Oh forget it, she would find those books herself.

It was hard for Elsa to pull down the steep ladder, but a few curses made it easier. Once at the top, she groped for the light switch and, shivering, drew the cardigan around her. The naked bulb gave off only a dim light, and Elsa needed some time to get used to the gloom.

She had not been up here for years. Most of the attic was empty. The odds and ends lying around did not take up even one-third of the space. There were two cupboards, shelves laden with empty flowerpots, books, and bottling jars, while on the floor lay several crates and cartons, a heavy wooden chest with iron fittings and several plastic bags with old drapes inside. Curious, Elsa looked around. She opened some of the cartons but saw immediately that they contained nothing that held her interest, only discarded clothes, worn-out shoes, old magazines, and medications that had passed their expiration date years ago. Good God, what junk Gertrud had hoarded! Elsa felt drawn to the old chest. Perhaps her mother's music was inside. If not, she would stop her search and wait until Gertrud was home again. The chest's lock was damaged, and the lid squeaked loudly as Elsa propped it up. Here, it seemed, was what she had been hunting for. Polonaises by Chopin – well, no, those were too difficult for her. She couldn't find the book of sonatinas, but finally put another book of music aside to take downstairs instead. Also in the chest were a few old records, which aroused her unbounded enthusiasm. Lauritz Melchior! Curt Bois! How grand! They would definitely have to acquire a gramophone so that they could listen again to their treasure trove. As she replaced the records, her groping hands discovered a large brown envelope at the bottom of the chest. Pulling it out, she saw to her surprise that it was sealed, with no address or other markings to suggest the nature of its contents.

Elsa hesitated briefly, then decided to take the envelope downstairs with her and placed it inside the music book. She made sure that she had not overlooked anything inside the chest and then closed the lid. With the book tucked under her left arm, she descended the ladder, clinging tightly to the banister with her other hand. Despite her impatience, she moved slowly and cautiously. Finally, she felt solid floor under her feet. She took a moment to catch her breath, and then, seized by an odd restlessness, went directly to the living room.

She put down the music book, turned on a lamp, got a letter opener and plopped herself down on the couch. After putting on her reading glasses, she opened the music book and removed the large envelope. She hesitated for a moment, undecided, then her curiosity won out. With a resolute motion she took the letter opener and slit open the envelope. Inside were three letters and an old photograph. Looking at the picture, Elsa recognized it as the same one that stood on the piano. It showed her mother, Salomon, Gertrud, and herself. Elsa smiled, amused. How she and her sister had idolized Salomon! He had been, without a doubt, the most handsome, the most charming stepfather one could imagine. Still smiling, she turned to the letters, but at once her good humor disappeared, and a frown creased her forehead as she recognized the unmistakable handwriting of her husband Curt, dead now for many years. She had always poked good-natured fun at his childlike handwriting. Only why were these letters addressed to her sister?

A curious feeling crept over her, and her heart began to beat faster. One of the envelopes bore only her sister's name, another was addressed to her sister's home, the last one showed an address in the city of Kiel. The postmarks were scarcely legible. It crossed her mind that one shouldn't read other people's letters, but if these letters were written by her husband and addressed to her sister, one surely could, for once, make an exception. With a gnawing sense of doing something forbidden, Elsa took all the letters out of their envelopes and looked for the one with the earliest date. It was dated August 21, 1938.

A glance at the heading left Elsa aghast. "My beloved Gertrud," it said in the familiar handwriting. "Beloved Gertrud? How on earth is he addressing her?" the words escaped from her throat as the hand holding the letter trembled slightly. As she continued reading, she felt that at this moment she had to be strong, forearmed against something that would be nearly unbearable.

My beloved Gertrud, do you know what day this is? Exactly one year ago we kissed for the first time. You wanted to pick Elsa and me up to go to Uncle Henry's birthday party. Elsa had run upstairs once more because she had forgotten her shawl and I was helping you put on your coat. We were standing in the hallway in front of the large mirror. I behind you with my hands on your shoulders. Your face was beaming at me and suddenly you turned and gave me a kiss, directly on my mouth. And then another one. I felt your body very close to mine. When you looked at me and that warm gaze from your doe-like eyes hit me, I was lost. All of a sudden I knew that I loved you. I felt as if I had been only consoling myself with Elsa, while in reality I was just waiting for you. I want to thank you for this wonderful year, for those unimaginable hours of love and tenderness, even if they were stolen moments. Tonight, during Uncle Henry's birthday party, we'll see each other again. I'll smuggle this brief letter into your pocket and hope we can find an opportunity to discuss when and where we'll meet the next time. Perhaps we can even kiss again. I always feel your lips upon mine. In two hours I shall see you again. I can hardly wait. With love, Curt.

Elsa let the letter drop in her lap. Her face had turned ashen. Something inside her refused to believe what she had just read. Surely her Curt could not have written that! It simply wasn't possible. She would have noticed something. Curt and Gertrud had been polite to one another, but they never seemed particularly friendly or even affectionate. Then it suddenly crossed her mind – this had been part of the deception. Perhaps they had acted so indifferently toward one another to divert suspicion. Distractedly she reached for the second letter, dated October 13, 1938, while her eyes slowly filled with tears.

My sweetheart! I am still so terribly confused. A week has passed since you told me the news. Isn't there still a chance that you are mistaken? I know Elsa isn't always regular and sometimes it comes late.

Elsa was weeping. She pressed her clenched fist against her breast and whispered brokenly: "For God's sake – he can't mean that Gertrud …"

Just wait for your next period, then see a doctor. Don't immediately assume the worst. We have to be more careful in the future. I love you so much. But I told you from the very beginning that we won't have a future together. You know why it's impossible for Elsa and me to separate. You are still so young, darling. You must not tie yourself down to me. Gertrud, please forgive this chaotic letter – you have to understand that ever since your first hints, I have been more than anxious. I love you, yours, Curt.

Elsa pulled a handkerchief out of her cardigan, took off her glasses and wiped her wet, reddened eyes. How could Curt have done this! He was always so loving and attentive. How terrible it had been for both of them when the doctor informed them, after the stillbirth, that Elsa must never become pregnant again. Solemnly Curt had promised that he would remain with her, that he would never leave her, even though he had always dreamed of having a large family. And indeed, he had kept his promise, Elsa thought bitterly, even if in his own way. She felt exhausted and drained as she took the last letter out of the envelope, replaced her glasses, and began to read the letter dated July 30, 1939.

Gertrud, in a few days Elsa and I will move to Freiburg. My son is already one month old, and I still haven't seen him, except for the photo that you sent Elsa. I'm very sad.

The handwriting was becoming blurred in her eyes. With a choked voice she blurted out the name of her nephew. Martin! That simply must not be true.

It has really hurt me that you've avoided me so constantly during the last few months. I can scarcely bear it. But I also know that I must not blame you in any way. Just as you hoped that I would be with you and our child, I have been bound by the promise that I made to Elsa. You have been admirably consistent. I implore you, most fervently, for only one thing: Don't deprive me of the boy entirely. Officially I am his uncle. Let me at least see him in that capacity from time to time. Gertrud, how long do you intend to stay in Kiel? Is there still a chance that I will see our child and you before I go to Freiburg? I would so much like to say farewell to you. If you need money, please let me know. I will do anything for you two, at least to the extent that you will let me. Love, your Curt.

Sadness enveloped Elsa like a giant wave that swept away everything in its path. She was scarcely able to cling to a single clear thought. Only, why had this happened to her? Had she not been a good wife to Curt? Why did Gertrud never tell her son who his father was? That his father was good Uncle Curt, to whom the boy felt so attached.

All these years living with Gertrud under one roof! How she had worried all the time about Gertrud and her weak heart. Suddenly, together with boundless sadness and disappointment, Elsa felt another emotion, a feeling that had formerly been alien to her: she felt hatred creeping into her heart. She pressed her fingertips against her temples. In her mind's eye she saw Gertrud, Curt, and Martin. Martin, the child that she and Curt had always wished for. Gertrud had the child, and she had taken away Elsa's husband. She had destroyed everything. Everything. Of what use now was the memory of Curt? None. Nothing at all remained. Elsa's stare was empty as she once more took off her glasses and placed them, together with the letters, on the living room table. "I hate you, Gertrud. You will pay for this," she whispered.

*****

"Do you want another piece of pie, my boy? Take all you want; there's plenty. And do you still have coffee in your cup?"

Expectantly Elsa looked at her nephew, who sat opposite her at the kitchen table.

"Yes, Aunt Elsa, I still have enough coffee. And I won't say no to your good apple pie."

It was the first time since Gertrud's funeral that Elsa and Martin had seen each other. Elsa pushed the third piece of apple pie onto his plate.

"I'm happy that you came to visit me. You've had a difficult year. First your accident, then Gertrud's sudden death. Things got to be too much for her."

Deep folds furrowed her brow as she continued sorrowfully, "It's still like a nightmare for me. I simply don't understand why she didn't use her nitroglycerin spray when she had the attack. She would have survived! And on that afternoon, of all days, I wasn't home."

In between biting off two morsels of pie, Martin was searching for the right words: "It's okay now, Aunt Elsa. You don't need to blame yourself. You told me that she had one bottle of that spray in her handbag and another one in the chest of drawers as always. The fact that she didn't make it that far and couldn't call for help – that had nothing to do with you. After all, you couldn't be with her twenty-four seven."

With a melancholy sigh, Elsa nodded in mild assent. Then she took another sip of coffee. "You're right, of course, Martin. I couldn't be with her all the time, but if I had been home, I could have helped her. That really gets me down."

"Let's not talk about her death anymore, Auntie. We can't bring her back to life no matter what," Martin clumsily tried to get her off the subject.

"You know, in fact I often wished that you and Uncle Curt – that you two had been my parents. Mom was okay, but she was always so nervous and restless. Besides it would have been so much nicer to have a mother *and* a father. I really missed having a father, believe me."

Elsa put down the coffee cup. "Well, at least I managed to convince Gertrud to send you to us now and again during vacations."

As Martin smiled, two dimples formed in his cheeks. Elsa scrutinized his face, searching for a resemblance to Curt. No, Curt did not have dimples.

"I still enjoy those memories." Martin's voice brought her back from her reverie. "It was a wonderful time. I remember how Uncle Curt played soccer with me and how we looked for mushrooms in the woods. And with you I could talk about anything. But that wasn't possible with mom. You should have seen how she blew her top when I asked her about my father. You couldn't squeeze anything at all out of her. Finally she simply wouldn't react anymore when I brought up the subject. I was quite mad at her, I tell you."

These memories awakened feelings of anger and helplessness in Martin.

"You're right," his aunt agreed, "she was determined to remain silent. I couldn't understand it either. We may have been five years apart in age, but we told each other everything, especially when we were young. After my marriage to Curt, we didn't see each other as often, of course, but that didn't really change anything. Still – not a single syllable about your father ever crossed her lips with me. Your mother was incredibly strong-willed. She didn't tell a soul about her pregnancy. After the Night of Broken Crystal, she went to Aunt Erna in Kiel and didn't come back. I heard from her again only during the summer of

174

'39. She sent me a photo of you. You were just a few days old. She wrote on the margin: "May I introduce you to your nephew Martin? He was born June 26th." That was all. Not a word about the identity of your father. Good God, how I worried about her. Okay, Aunt Erna was a sensible woman, but I still worried, especially about Gertrud's state of mind."

"Didn't you have some idea back then about who my father might be?" Martin asked. He had posed this question to his aunt many times and always received the same unsatisfying answer. Nevertheless he continued to ask, reviving a fragment of the past in which he had played an important role. Occasionally he admitted to himself that this was really enough for him and that he had long ago given up ever learning who his father had been.

"I've also wracked my brains about that, Martin. It could have happened when she was at Aunt Erna's for a few days, before she moved to Kiel permanently. Later on, I confronted her about this, but she only shrugged her shoulders and said that it was nobody's business. Stubborn as a mule! And yet I felt sorry for her. She wasn't even twenty when she had you. She had had many bad experiences before she went to Kiel. She suffered especially because of all the things that were happening to Salomon. Of course, that upset me too, but I was living with Curt and didn't hear much about it."

Elsa's thoughts wandered to the photo on the piano, which showed the small family, so happy at one time. Martin followed her gaze and said, "she also didn't say much about your stepfather. I asked her sometimes to tell me about those days. What it was like for Salomon when he was no longer allowed to practice his profession because he was a Jew, how your mother could ever have been capable of abandoning him." Martin's cheeks reddened slightly. With this subject he was right in his element.

"Well, she didn't quite abandon Salomon," Elsa contradicted him. "In the beginning she stuck by him, but when he was no longer allowed to practice it must have become more and more unbearable for her. They had hardly any money left. The repressive measures increased week by week. Mother told me at the time that they would probably get a divorce. She had heard that it was possible to get a divorce for racial reasons, and she considered this seriously as a way to save her skin. Gertrud and I despised her because of her weakness. But, it didn't get to a divorce after all. Gertrud experienced all that far more intensely than I because she lived with both of them under one roof."

"I was so incredibly interested in all that. But she absolutely did not want to speak about it. She always said that those times had been so horrible that she didn't ever want to remember them. And then she would change the subject. Even though she wasn't a bad person, there were things about her which I simply did not understand. At the time I considered her completely impossible. Then somewhere along the line, I simply stopped asking her questions and if I avoided certain subjects like Salomon, for example, I could get along with her quite well." Martin sighed.

Elsa nodded in sympathy, lost in her thoughts. "Yes, it's true, Gertrud was particularly sensitive in all matters concerning Salomon. She was very attached to him. Both of us were, but she of course went through the really terrible times with him. He could have saved himself, if he had emigrated in time, but he waited too long. He was such a cultured person and was so well regarded that he couldn't imagine that things could get even worse. He always hoped for a miracle.

I'll never forget the day we all saw him for the last time. Just by chance I was present when they came to take him away. On October 27, 1938, at seven o'clock in the evening. Two of them came. A policeman in uniform and a man in civilian clothes. We had just eaten dinner. Salomon had to sign a document that confirmed his deportation to Poland, and then he had to go with them at once. He was permitted to take along only a small suitcase with clothes and toiletries. Within just two days about 17, 000 Polish Jews were deported, along with stateless persons who had come to Germany from territories belonging to Poland. Salomon was one of them. Just imagine: although he was not a German citizen, at that time Salomon had been in Germany for more than twenty years. The problem was that Poland didn't want these people either. I recall that Gertrud carried on like a mad woman. It was bad for me, too. You know how much we liked Salomon. Mother sat at the table, petrified, and stared out the window. It was horrible."

Overcome by memories, Elsa covered her face with both hands and slightly rocked her head back and forth.

Martin tactfully remained silent for a few moments. "I can't understand why you two never talked about those times later on. Surely there was so much to get off your chest and it would have helped to talk about it."

Only now did Elsa slip her hands from her face. She stared fixedly at her coffee cup. She too was moved deeply by these conversations.

"I think so too, Martin. Your mother and I lived together for so many years. After Curt's death, I received a good pension, but your mother had very little money. Since both of us were now alone, it made sense to move in together, but we rarely talked about old times. Ever since she was pregnant with you and went to Kiel, she shut herself off from me. To be honest, there were times when I secretly admired how she managed to keep the entire world from knowing who your father was. She was without a doubt incredibly strong. One mustn't forget how young she was at the time. When your Uncle Curt took a position in Freiburg shortly before the war, I would have liked to take her and you with us. But Gertrud didn't want to. She wanted to stay with Aunt Erna in Kiel."

"Did you ever try to find out from Aunt Erna who could have been my father? Perhaps mom told her everything," Martin mused halfheartedly.

Elsa shrugged her shoulders. "I don't know whether Gertrud confided in Aunt Erna. Of course, she was your godmother, but I don't know whether she knew anything. After she died in 1941, there was absolutely no one around anymore who could have given me some information. Except your mother, of course, but she didn't want to."

Elsa bent down and looked at Martin's empty cup. She reached for the coffee pot and looked inquiringly at her nephew. Martin shook his head nearly imperceptibly with a frustrated, almost bitter smile.

"No, Aunt Elsa, I've had enough coffee for today. You know what I'll do now? I'll take a good book and sit in the garden for a bit."

Elsa recalled the real reason her nephew had come to visit. "And when do you want to look over your mother's things and decide what you want to take with you to Munich? Till now I've left everything the way it was, but I'd like to start sorting things out."

Cautiously, Martin stood up. Since his accident his body movements were rather uncertain. "I'll start soon. For the moment I'll go outside, if you don't mind. I'm going to rummage around a bit more tomorrow. As you know I'm not driving back before the afternoon, so that gives me another half day."

Martin had almost reached the kitchen door when he stopped and turned around. "Oh, I just remembered." With a smile, he reached down into the pocket of his jacket and took out an envelope. "This is a letter from mom that has been lying around my house for God knows how many years."

Like a white dove the letter fluttered before her nose and then landed in front of her on the table. "That was really an eternity ago. When I was still married and Eva was so ill, mom was with us for awhile."

Lost in thought, Elsa reached for the envelope. "Yes, yes, that happened the year before we moved in together. The letter is for me? Do you know what it says?"

"No. She put it into my hand and said I should keep it. It was intended for you, and I was to give it to you in case she died before you. If you died before her, I was to give it back to her. Okay, Auntie, there it is. I'm going outside in the sun now. See you later."

Then, in a slightly sarcastic tone, he added: "And if it happens to contain the grand revelation of who my father is, you'll let me know, won't you?"

Elsa kept silent and followed her nephew with her eyes. No, she would never tell him that Curt was his father. That was none of his business. He hadn't known it for more than fifty years and there was no reason he should learn it at this late date. He would only ask unpleasant questions that would embarrass her and conjure up the past. For another minute Elsa sat motionless before she got ready to open the envelope. Well, yet another letter. She hadn't had good experiences with letters lately. She put on her glasses. With a combination of curiosity and foreboding she slit open the envelope with a fruit knife that was lying on the table. The letter was dated August 4, 1972, and took up several pages. Like all her sister's letters, it was written in brown ink.

Dear Elsa, I've decided to leave this letter for you with Martin. When you read it, I won't be living anymore. First of all I would like to thank you for always being on my side, even at times when it certainly was not easy for you. I know that you were disappointed that I never told you who Martin's father was. In earlier times we told each other everything, and I knew that if I didn't take you into my confidence it might well spoil our relationship. But I felt myself bound by the promise that I gave to the man whom I loved more than anyone and whom you loved as well.

Elsa took off her glasses and massaged her throbbing temples. If she had not loved him, she would never have become his wife. Yes it was true, she had loved Curt beyond all measure, even if he apparently had not deserved it. Sighing, she put on her glasses again and continued reading.

He captivated us from the very moment mother introduced him to us. Do you still remember when we decided that we had the best and most handsome stepfather in the entire world?

The handwriting began to dance before Elsa's eyes and no longer made sense. She had to reread the last paragraph. It was utterly out of the question. Gertrud surely couldn't mean Salomon. Not Salomon, it wasn't possible! Her mouth opened in a silent outcry, her eyes wide with terror. Elsa forced herself to keep on reading

181

and at the same time dug her teeth into the back of her left hand.

How we both adored him! And he certainly didn't mind it at all. Later my feelings toward him began to bewilder me. The crush of an adolescent girl slowly turned into something else. At one time I was about to tell you that I had fallen in love with him. But I was ashamed. After all, Salomon was like a father to us. And you had just fallen in love with your Curt, and one couldn't talk to you about anything else. For a long time Salomon didn't notice my feelings. He had other worries. His situation worsened from year to year and, as a result, for all of us. But during the summer of '38 he also fell in love with me. Living with mother had become unbearable, and we felt it was only a question of time until she would leave him. I would have done anything for him. We tried to console and help one another. All that was complicated by our constant fear that mother or someone else would notice something. A Polish Jew and his stepdaughter – that would have been wonderful grist for their mills. People denounced you for far less than that. Shortly before his deportation I found out that I was pregnant. Salomon had become completely despondent. He no longer believed that we could have a future together. In case something should happen, he asked me to promise that I would never tell anyone that he was the child's father. The child of a Jew would have to undergo too much suffering. He wanted his child to have the chance to grow up Christian. With a Christian mother that would be no problem. The child was to be bap-

tized. I gave him that promise. And now, Elsa, your Curt becomes involved. During the summer I once found myself near his institute and on the spur of the moment I decided to visit him and say hello. His secretary wasn't there, so I marched straight into his office. I didn't knock first. And there those two stood wildly kissing each other. They hadn't even heard me come in. Only when I cleared my throat did they jump apart. Miss Meiser, her face as red as a beet, immediately left the office.

Stunned, Elsa let the letter drop into her lap. That nice, sweet Miss Meiser? This simply couldn't be true. A few moments earlier she had felt a sense of jubilation stirring, at first hesitantly, then more freely. Curt was not Martin's father. He had been faithful to her. That alone was important. But now … a large tear detached itself slowly from the corner of her eye and dropped onto the letter.

Curt began to offer some sort of explanation, but I waved it aside and went out. But after Salomon was deported, I hit upon an idea. I wanted to honor the spirit of his wishes and to find an Aryan father for the child, which I expected within a few months. I also knew that at some point it might be necessary to have proof of that fatherhood and I would need proof if anyone should denounce me for having had an affair with a Jew. I had Curt in the palm of my hand. I went to his institute again and explained to him that I needed his help. If he refused, I would tell you about his relationship with Miss Meiser. I asked him to write me three letters indicating that he was the father of my child. To make sure that everything happened as I had planned, I had decided to write the letters myself. Curt was then to copy them in his own handwriting. I brought the first two letters along when I visited him the first time. Curt hardly resisted. His guilt concerning you was simply too great. I waited for an hour in his office while he copied the letters. One of the envelopes I put in my pocket, the other I put in the mailbox myself. I mailed the third letter to his institute after Martin's birth, telling Curt to mail his handwritten copy to me in Kiel. He may have gnashed his teeth, but he stuck to our agreement. I never told him why he had to pretend to be Martin's father. When he asked me I simply brought up Miss Meiser. I was surprised myself how well it all worked out.

The crash was so loud and unexpected that Elsa uttered a high-pitched cry and clutched at her heart. Two small spray bottles had been banged with great force on the table. In utter confusion Elsa stared directly into the incensed eyes of her nephew.

"Good God, my boy, how you've startled me." Elsa's pulse was racing as she looked up, anxious and frightened, and realized that Martin's face was only a few inches away from her own.

"The sun has disappeared again. So I decided to start looking through mother's belongings right away."

Sweat glistened on Martin's forehead. He spoke fast and excitedly.

"Just look, Aunt Elsa, I found mom's bottles with the nitroglycerin spray. Exactly as you said, one in the chest-of-drawers, the other in a handbag."

Elsa swallowed nervously and, with trembling hands, sought support from the edge of the table.

Suddenly tears appeared in Martin's eyes as he explained:

"Auntie, mom never had a chance. She must have forgotten to get the spray refilled."

Misinterpreting her tears of relief, he laid his forehead against hers and added feelingly "See, even if you had been home when she had the attack, you couldn't have helped her. Poor mom!"

Ice Cream or Pudding

"K-e-e-vin, lunch!"

"Yeah."

The computer game is terminated, the computer shut down. Then heavy steps come thundering down the stairs. When Kevin enters the dining room, his parents are already sitting at the table. The boy sits down at his seat, reaches for the soda bottle and fills his glass. Greedily and without pausing he empties it and immediately refills it. His mother takes the bottle from his hand and pours soda for her husband and herself.

A heavy piece of pizza lands on Kevin's plate; the crust is thick and white. Pepperoni slices cling to pieces of ham; the aroma of oregano fills the air.

"Yum, pizza, super!"

Kevin stuffs his mouth; the cheese stretches into long strings; his hands are covered with grease. Silence. Relaxed and mute, they munch away intently. A second bottle of soda makes the round. Dad belches loudly; Mom throws him a reproachful glance. Kevin smirks.

The next slice is not quite as hot, but still tastes good. Kevin chows down greedily.

"What's for dessert?"

"Ice cream or pudding, whichever you want."

"Chocolate pudding?"

"Yes, with vanilla sauce. And you?"

Mom is turning to her husband.

"Ice cream."

He drinks down the contents of his glass. She gets up, laboriously piles the dishes in stacks and carries them into the kitchen. She waddles along; her thighs rub together with every step, making a swishing sound.

"Take the glasses into the kitchen," dad says. Kevin's face takes on a sullen expression, but he does what he is told. His mother returns with a tray. A half-filled bottle of caraway liquor, two small glasses, two dishes with different colored scoops of ice cream, an aerosol can of whipped cream, a plastic cup of chocolate pudding with vanilla cream, three teaspoons. Huffing and puffing she puts the tray down. Dad reaches for one of the dishes of ice cream, sprays a mountain of whipped cream on it and spoons it down with enjoyment. Mom does likewise. Kevin is still chewing as he sits down once more at the table. While in the kitchen he has stuffed his mouth with jelly beans. He now tears the silver foil from the pudding cup and laughs at the erupting noise, then spreads thick rings of whipped cream on top of the vanilla sauce.

"Sounds like a fart," he says, laughing. His father snorts and reaches for his cigarettes, while his mother eats with gusto. When she has gulped down the contents of the dish, she pours a glass of liquor for her husband

and herself. They say cheers to each other before downing the liquor.

"Aaaah. That feels good. Helps the digestion."

"A little midday nap," Kevin's father announces happily, patting his wife's thigh and getting up. He doesn't bother to close the top button of his pants. His belly is so ample that one can't see the button anyway. Mom looks at the clock.

"At half-past three Barbara is coming for coffee."

Kevin raises his face.

"Are we going to have cake?" he asks expectantly.

"Of course," his mother replies. "Apple tarts and nut cake."

"Cool!" Kevin says.

He is feeling lazy and undecided what to do until then. He finished his homework on Saturday, the day before. Today he is loafing. The dishes are in the dishwasher; his parents have disappeared into the bedroom. Kevin slouches down on the couch and grabs the remote control. He soon loses interest in channel surfing. Before going to his room, he gets a bag of licorice from a drawer in the living room buffet and then awkwardly climbs up the stairs. As he plays his computer game, he mechanically stuffs the licorice into his mouth.

Shortly after 3:30 the doorbell rings. Kevin hears his Aunt Barbara greeting his father and mother. A bit later they all sit around the dining room table. Barbara watches Kevin gulp down a third piece of nut cake and turns her worried face toward his parents.

"It's just a half-year more," she says between two bites of apple tarts. "You should begin to pay attention."

"Half a year is a long time," Dad says, eating. Mom remains silent. When Kevin reaches for a fourth piece of nut cake, his mother throws him a warning glance.

"One more and that's it."

"But Mom!"

"That's it, I said!"

Kevin sighs and struggles up the stairs again to his computer.

"Don't you dare!"

Mom lightly slaps Kevin's hand which is reaching for a cookie.

"Mom, pleeease!"

Frustrated, Kevin sticks out his lower lip and whines. He whimpers like a baby, whom one has inexplicably deprived of his nipple.

"No arguments."

His mother shows a stern face; his father shovels peanuts into his mouth. She removes the cookie jar from Kevin's reach and says reproachfully:

"There are only two months left. You really have to exert yourself."

Kevin is fighting back tears. He crosses his lower arms on the table and slowly lowers his head until his forehead rests on one of his arms. His mother hears his loud sighs and the crunching noises of her husband's chewing as he watches TV.

"Are you going to drive Kevin or should I?"

"You go ahead. This is really interesting right now."

Her husband stays glued to the TV. She struggles to get up and puts one hand on Kevin's shoulder.

"Come on."

"I don't feel like it." His voice sounds close to crying.

"I know, but come on. We've got to. Just a little while more and we'll be all done, right?"

With a trace of tenderness she strokes his forehead. His shoulders slumping, Kevin drags himself to the coat closet, puts on his sneakers, and reaches for his parka. He follows his mother to the VW and sits down on the passenger side. It's a short drive. She stops on the side of the road after about three miles. Her boy struggles tortuously out of his seat, noisily slams the door shut, and follows the car with his eyes until it disappears from sight. Then he starts out.

When he arrives home he is sweaty and out of breath. His mother is sitting on the living room couch next to his father.

"Now just a short quarter of an hour on the bicycle, and you'll be all done for today."

She smiles at him encouragingly as he takes off his parka. They have brought the home-trainer up from the basement and installed it in the living room so that they can watch while he pedals. This way he can't put one over on them. The voices from the television drown out the humming of the bicycle, a swelling or diminishing noise, all depending on how hard Kevin is stepping on the pedals. After five minutes he wants to stop.

"I can't go on," he laments.

"Ten minutes more," his mother says and looks at the clock. She does not give in. Kevin's heart is racing as he gets off the bicycle with trembling knees. Sweat is running down his body; he is panting.

After taking a shower, he is sitting on the couch next to his mother in his pajamas. She has slung one arm around his shoulder; his tired head rests against her large breast. On the table in front of them stands a bottle of mineral water for Kevin. She herself is drinking a coke, her husband a beer.

"Time for bed," Kevin's father says, looking at the clock. His mother withdraws her arm and reaches for the cheese puffs. Kevin swallows, watching her shove the snack into her mouth, one handful after the other.

"I want some too."

"You've brushed your teeth already. Up you go to bed. If you want to, you can drink some more water."

"I'm hungry!"

"You've got to wait until breakfast." Her voice suddenly turns soft. She feels sorry for the boy.

"You know that's the way it's got to be," she adds tenderly. They wish each other good night, and Kevin goes to his room. He wants to turn on the computer and play a few minutes more, but he can scarcely keep his eyes open.

"Good grief, we won't make it. It's just one more week," his mother laments, "and he still weighs four pounds too much."

"Well, then we'll just have to give him laxatives and diuretics every day after school." Dad is satisfied with his idea.

The week passes rather slowly. Kevin cries a lot. He often feels dizzy. Once he has a sudden attack of weakness in the schoolyard. His mother picks him up from school. Nevertheless he has to jog and bicycle the very same day. Every morning they relax their efforts a bit, when they observe that the pills have had the desired effect.

Finally the hour has come.

In the morning Kevin slips into his jeans, which have become too wide for him, and tightens the belt. He is ill from all the excitement. Will all those efforts pay off? This morning he can't eat a thing. It feels as though he has rocks in his stomach.

His appointment is at eleven. The day before, his mother made it a point to go to her hairdresser. She is even more nervous than Kevin and eats twice as much as usual in order to calm down. At half past ten they get into the VW and drive to the Office of Public Health. It's hard to find a place to park.

Mom goes with Kevin to the registration desk and turns in a form. Extra chairs have been placed in the corridor. Many children, accompanied mainly by their mothers, populate the hallway. They are all the same age, but their weights differ.

Nearly an hour later Kevin's name is called. Fearfully he enters a room with his mother. A woman physician, dressed in a white smock, approaches and shakes hands with them while asking about the results of the thyroid exam, which they had to bring along. She quickly glances at it, murmurs "that's fine," and asks Kevin to strip down to his underwear. His heart is racing as she measures his height and then proceeds to weigh him. After that he can dress again. The doctor sits down at her desk and makes herself some notes. Kevin's mother can scarcely control herself any longer; her breath comes heavily, and she presses a fist against her breast. Her body is completely tense. Kevin sits next to her, pale and fearful. Both stare at the doctor as though transfixed.

"You were lucky," she says. "To be sure, your son is still overweight, but he registers two pounds below the limit."

Kevin's mother sighs with relief and, her face shining, presses Kevin to herself. Tears shimmer in her eyes. Her son utters a shout of pure joy and with a cheer, throws his arms in the air. Then, laughing, he returns his mother's embrace.

"Well, let's take a look," says the doctor and leafs through her documents, comparing Kevin's figures with various tables and then announcing:

"Beginning next month Kevin's contributions to his health insurance go up by 3%. In addition you, together with your son, must attend a course about healthy nutrition here at the Office of Public Health. Get a certificate that both of you have attended the course. You will need it for your next appointment two years from now. Your husband, incidentally, is also welcome to participate. It always makes the most sense if the whole family works together on this."

The physician shuts her workbook, gets up and says goodbye to mother and son.

"You really were lucky," she adds. "This morning I already had to tell five families that they are forfeiting custody."

As Kevin and his mother leave the office building, they are beside themselves with joy and relief.

"And what should we do now?" asks Kevin, still in seventh heaven.

"Now we are going to celebrate," his mother says. "There's an ice cream parlor just down the street."

The Tiny Christmas Bell

Once upon a time there was a tiny little bell, scarcely bigger than a thimble. Like many other little bells, tree lights, and many colored ornaments, it hung down from a large fir tree, festively decorated for the holiday. On the top of the tree reigned a golden-haired angel. Christmas Eve was just a few days away. The beautiful Christmas tree stood squarely in the middle of the market place of a small city and radiated a festive glow. When it snowed, a thousand tiny snowflakes came to rest on the outspread arms of the tree, and the tree lights, bells, and colored ornaments looked as if they were covered with an icing made of sugar.

Many of the folks in that small town were so busy with their Christmas shopping that they passed by the beautiful tree without paying it any attention. But others stopped and looked at it with admiration, because it was truly so lovely to see.

Lisa, too, stopped every day in front of the tree and enjoyed the wonderful sight. On her way to school she had to cross the market place and again on her way home. Sometimes the wind made the branches rock softly back and forth, and then Lisa had the feeling that the tree was nodding to her like an old friend. She had been looking at it very carefully and had tried to count all those tree lights, bells, and ornaments. But as she counted, she did not realize that she had overlooked one bell. Because it was so tiny and hidden at the very top of the tree, no one could see it. That bell was much smaller than all the other bells, but it was especially beautiful. Its color glittered in a warm shade of gold, and it hung from a dark red velvet ribbon, whose borders were magnificently embroidered. None of the other bells noticed it because it was so tiny, and not one of them could have explained how it had reached that height way up in the air. Even our little bell couldn't have told you. As long as it could remember, it had lain in a dark box. And suddenly – it didn't really know what was happening that day – it had been taken out of the box and hung by its small velvet ribbon way up high on the tree. It only remembered a man on a ladder and two hands. When it looked downward later, it became terribly frightened. It was hanging so high that it became dizzy, and it was even a bit worried that it might fall down.

After a while, it became aware that from up there one had an especially fine view, and it curiously observed the goings-on in the marketplace. And when it looked down, it noticed a little girl who passed the tree twice a day. She had flaxen hair that had been braided into a thick pigtail, and wonderful blue eyes, which looked admiringly at the tree each day. After she had stood there for a while, holding her little head slightly at an angle, she skipped happily away, holding tightly to her red school bag. The tiny bell often looked down at the little girl and tried to get her attention. But the ringing of the bell was so delicate and soft that Lisa could not possibly hear it.

The tiny bell felt so lonely. It certainly did not feel like landing in a dark box again after a few weeks, where it would have to spend an entire year once more. If it could only climb down to that little girl! It would then chime as sweetly as it knew how, and it was sure that the girl would be very pleased. But how to get down? The tiny bell thought about it for hours and suddenly had an idea. As sweetly as possible it smiled at the angel with the golden hair. After all, he was so close to the tiny bell, there, at the highest tip of the tree. It swung back and forth and chimed as loudly as it could. Very much surprised, the angel looked down at it. Not a breeze was stirring at the moment, so how then could a bell be ringing?

The tiny bell gathered up every bit of its courage and beamed at the angel.

"May I ask you something?" it cried out as loudly as possible.

The angel bowed down. He could scarcely understand the tiny bell, and what he heard was hardly more than a whisper. The angel bent down even more.

"I'd like to ask you something," the tiny bell repeated and strained its voice almost to the breaking point. An amused smile spread across the angel's pale, handsome face.

"What do you want to ask me?" he answered in a soft voice.

"There is a girl down there with a blond pigtail and a red school bag. That little girl looks so sweet, and she stops twice a day before our tree and looks at it very closely," the tiny bell shouted. The friendly smile of the angel encouraged it to go on. It took a deep breath and shouted: "I would like so much to be with that little girl. I believe she would be very happy with me if I came down to her."

"Well," the angel said, "this is possible, of course. But what did you want to ask me?"

The throat of the tiny bell was beginning to hurt, but it bravely kept on shouting.

"When she stands in front of the tree again, could you perhaps come down to me and untie me from the branch? And then could you throw me down into the snow?" The tiny bell paused for a moment. "But do it very carefully, so I don't get hurt," it added, a bit more softly.

It felt a slight shudder from the treetop and saw that it was caused by the laughter of the angel. He is making fun of me, thought the tiny bell, and became very sad.

"Well, you certainly are a brave little thing," the angel said, laughing. Worried, the tiny bell gazed upward and looked into the kind eyes of the angel. It smiled timidly. "Such courage must be rewarded," the angel went on, chuckling. "All right, I'll help you; when the little girl comes back, ring as hard as you can. Then I will climb down to you and untie the ribbon from the twig. But I have to warn you: if the girl doesn't find you when you are

down below, I won't be able to help you anymore. I won't be able to lift you up here again."

The tiny bell gratefully beamed at the angel.

"That is so kind of you. That's exactly what we will do."
The hours passed. Slowly evening fell. It got dark and cool, and the tiny bell knew that this would be its last night upon the Christmas tree. It was so excited that it could scarcely sleep and nervously chimed all to itself.

The next morning the time had come. As usual, Lisa stopped in front of the tree on her way to school. It had snowed during the night, and the tiny bell worried that its cover of snow might be so heavy that the angel would not be able to hear its chimes and shouts. But all went well. As soon as the tiny bell caught sight of Lisa, it swung madly back and forth and shouted to the angel. He nimbly climbed down from branch to branch and swiftly arrived at the side of the tiny bell.

"Hurry, hurry," said the tiny bell, all out of breath, "or she will be gone!"

It felt the ribbon being untied from the branch and suddenly it was afraid. The tree was so tall. What if it broke into a thousand pieces when it hit the ground? It was just about to tell the angel that it had thought it over one more time, when it was already being tossed away from the tree in a high and wide arc.

"Good luck," it heard the angel say, as it fell and fell.

The angel's aim had been perfect and the tiny bell landed with a little plop in the soft snow, exactly at Lisa's feet. The girl bent down and curiously dug into the small hole which the tiny bell had made in the snow. With a joyful cry she fished it out by the velvet ribbon. What a wonderful tiny bell it was! Lisa laughed gaily and lovingly pressed it against her cheek. The tiny bell was nearly beside itself, and for a brief moment it was mute with joy.

"You will be my good luck charm from now on," Lisa whispered sweetly. "I will always carry you with me, always." And then she pressed a kiss on the tiny bell, which, out of sheer joy and happiness, started to chime.

GUY STERN, the translator, was born in 1922 in Hildesheim, Germany. From 1942 to 1945 he served in the US Army, Military Intelligence Service (rank of Master Sergeant). He was decorated with the Bronze Star. In 1953 he received his Ph.D. from Columbia University. Stern taught at various U.S. universities (most recently at Wayne State University) and as guest professor at German institutions. He was Interim Director of the Holocaust Memorial Center Zekelman Family Campus in Farmington Hills, MI, and is currently Director of its Institute of the Righteous. Beyond his publications on literature, he has translated dramas by Brecht and poems by contemporary German authors.